"Alex, about last night..."

Alain began speaking hesitantly as soon as the waiter had left.

It was what she'd been dreading. A postmortem. Now was the time to pretend a sophistication she was far from feeling.

"I think it's for the best if we both forget it—don't you?" she asked brightly.

"I certainly think we should start afresh," he agreed, to her relief. "If only because last night, I gave you the impression that I wanted to be your lover."

Disappointment surged through her. He wanted to assure her he wouldn't sully whatever remained of their working relationship—that he didn't want to mix business with pleasure.

"Alex..." He reached across and took her hand. "The truth is, I want more than that. I want you to marry me."

Angela Wells left the bustling world of media marketing and advertising to marry and start a family in a suburb of London. Writing started out as a hobby, and she uses backgrounds she knows well from her many travels for her books. Her ambitions, she says, in addition to writing many more romances, are to visit Australia, pilot a light aircraft and own a word-processing machine.

Books by Angela Wells

HARLEQUIN ROMANCE

HARLEQUIN PRESENTS

Don't miss any of our special offers. Write to us at the following address for information on our newest releases.

Harlequin Reader Service
P.O. Box 1397, Buffalo, NY 14240
Canadian address: P.O. Box 603,
Fort Erie, Ont. L2A 5X3

ENDLESS SUMMER
Angela Wells

Harlequin Books

TORONTO • NEW YORK • LONDON
AMSTERDAM • PARIS • SYDNEY • HAMBURG
STOCKHOLM • ATHENS • TOKYO • MILAN

Original hardcover edition published in 1990
by Mills & Boon Limited

ISBN 0-373-03167-X

Harlequin Romance first edition December 1991

ENDLESS SUMMER

CHAPTER ONE

IT WASN'T a good day to be returning to work after a week's absence caused by the assault on her auto-immune system by a VUO. Alex lowered her blonde head against the unwelcome force of the cold March wind, glad for the comfort of her calf-length pure wool top coat as she struggled up Lombard Street in the cold light of the early London morning.

Strange, she pondered, how, the more medical research progressed, the less it discovered it knew! Once what she had been suffering from would have been termed the common cold. Now it was solemnly diagnosed as a Virus of Unknown Origin! Either way there was still no known cure for it except time, or, as her doctor father was wont to say—'The only way past is through!' All of which was of little comfort to her at that moment as she wondered fleetingly if perhaps she shouldn't have taken a few more days off as the cold air nipped at her ears.

Almost certainly she should have worn the angora Balaclava which had been one of her Christmas presents, she allowed, smiling at her own vanity which decreed her appearance should always be in keeping with the elegant ambience of the French merchant bank where she worked as a researcher. Somehow the idea of stepping over such an august threshold dressed like a potential bank robber savoured too much of the ridiculous...

Still, once she was inside its imposing portals she'd be warm enough, especially as she intended to start the day with a cup of the delicious coffee the management provided for their employees in the staff lounge. First of all she'd check what messages had been left for her and any updating of information on the open files which had been done in her absence.

Relaxing as she reached her destination, entering by the staff door with her own personal key, and savouring the change of atmosphere, she walked swiftly through to the large office she shared with her assistant, Simone. It was far too early for the younger girl to have put in an appearance, of course, so she'd have the place to herself while she brought herself up to date.

She knew she was wrong the moment she stepped over the threshold. The long legs of the man seated in front of her VDU prevented him from facing it. Instead he was sitting side on, the same splendid limbs clothed in closely tailored silver-grey mohair, the gleam of which declaimed its quality as opposed to its wear! Alex paused in astonishment. A complete stranger? At this time of the morning—and apparently intent on gaining access to her meticulously compiled records?

'Can I help you?' she asked coolly, fixing him with the impersonal stare that she reserved for moments when she felt it necessary to hold her normal cheerful personality in check.

The unexpected occupant had neither said nor done anything to put her on guard, but his very presence there was a threat. Through every cell of her convalescent body she sensed it, as her quick eye absorbed the pristine white shirt, the maroon and silver tie, the hand-sewn lapels and individually cut and sewn buttonholes of his jacket— a sure sign of bespoke tailoring. A talented amateur dressmaker herself, she had a fine eye for such exquisite detail.

'Good morning.' He rose to his feet, the courtesy of his greeting chiding her uncompromising approach. 'I do hope so. I need urgent information about our dealings with Triple I. The file appears to be guarded.'

'Really?' Alex slipped her coat from her shoulders, conscious of impatient, heavy-lidded eyes the colour of oloroso sherry following her every movement as she walked a few paces to the neat wardrobe at one side of the room. She took her time in selecting a hanger, as her mind raced through the possibilities. He was no sneak thief. Everything about him suggested he was at home in the high-powered business of merchant banking. Everything from the plain gold watch on his left wrist, to the arrogant bearing of his dark head on those broad shoulders.

Yet the fact remained he hadn't been here a week ago and details of Triple I were classified as top secret, only she and her immediate superior Monsieur Delacroix knowing the access code she had used, although there was a complicated fail-safe system available in the case of disaster befalling either of them . . .

The archetypal yuppie, she decided, having put her coat away tidily. Early thirties probably, very sure of himself. One of the beautiful people, a flat in Knightsbridge, a Porsche and a blithe expectation that the world was not only his oyster but that it would offer him pearls at a mere command. She knew the type well—too well. Obviously new intake into the department intent on making an impression. Why else should he be here so early? Despite the fact that she admired such in-itiative, it wasn't going to be indulged at her expense!

Frustration at being thwarted firstly by an inanimate computer and then by an animate woman was now clearly to be read on his face as she met his gaze. On a countenance less structurally pleasing Alex would have called his expression malevolent, as contemptuously narrowed eyes travelled the length of her body, now conservatively clad in an emerald-green, long-sleeved cardigan suit, its lined skirt skimming her slim but shapely contours with understated flattery.

'Well?' he demanded edgily. 'Are you going to tell me the code or not?'

'That depends,' Alex met his deepening hostility with composure, 'on whether you're authorised to know it. Your name is?' She raised her lightly defined brows enquiringly, nearly certain he wouldn't be, but prepared to check rather than make a fool of herself.

'Dougal!' Dark, normally well-spaced brows met above a straight, assertive nose as his voice deepened to a growl.

Scottish, then? She thought she'd detected an accent underlying his clipped English, but then, with her wretched sinuses still partly blocked and slightly impeding the sharpness of her hearing she hadn't been certain.

'Right.' Returning to the keyboard, she demanded a list of authorised personnel feeling a quiet satisfaction when the name he'd given her did not appear.

'Sorry, Dougal.' She smiled up at him. 'Your name hasn't been added to the short-list. Why don't you go and get a coffee? Monsieur Delacroix will be here in fifteen minutes or so, and you can discuss the matter with him, but I'm afraid the odds are against you. If you'd been eligible to access the file you would already have been given your own code. And now, if you'll excuse me, I have a lot of work to catch up with.'

Resolutely she returned her attention to the screen, aware from the prickling sensation teasing her spine that Dougal's bad-tempered amber eyes continued to bore into her. Bother the man! She'd have to forsake her original idea of coffee. Heaven knew what he'd get up to if she left him alone in the office. Supposing he hit on her password by chance? She'd selected it because it was one she knew she'd never forget—but it hadn't been extraordinary. If he knew there was only a four character alphabetic field... A qualm of disquiet added to her discomfort. There was a determination about his bearing which suggested he was a poor and infrequent loser! The thought was horrifying. All the good will she'd built up over the years would disappear in an electronic flash!

It came as no surprise when he refused to take her broad hint to go away, asking instead in a low voice which trembled with some suppressed emotion she didn't care to evaluate, 'And your name is?'

'Alex, Alex Hammond.'

'And you've worked here for how long?'

'Oh, several years—long enough to know the rules!' She forced herself to smile pleasantly. After all, she loved her job and it was a very happy office. Far be it for her to make ructions with the newcomer.

'Then you'd better make the most of your job while you've still got it!'

'I beg your pardon?' Surely she hadn't heard him aright. 'Are you trying to threaten me?'

'Forget the *trying* Miss Hammond! I *am* threatening you!' The positive feel of his hands on her shoulders did nothing to assuage the shiver that traversed her spine. 'I'm tired of playing games. If you don't key me into the system by the time I count to five, then your long-standing association with the Banque de Varcennes will be terminated with the speed of a descending *guillotine* blade!'

'You're an industrial spy!' Alex shot to her feet, heart pounding, determined not to give an inch, some isolated part of her mind lecturing her that she really should have taken another day in bed. Fool that she was, not to have guessed what he was up to and sounded the alarm...

Somehow she hadn't judged him as being potentially violent, and even now, with his simmering anger a powerful aura surrounding him, she couldn't believe he really meant to injure her.

'One...two...three...' He paused, eyes narrowed speculatively as she faced him aghast. 'You can't be that out of touch, surely, that my name means nothing to you?'

'The only Dougal I've ever heard of was a dog in a television programme for children!' she defended herself almost hysterically. 'Oh, and I believe there was a farmer in a Scottish soap...oh, Monsieur Delacroix, thank heaven!'

The door had opened and to her relief Alex found herself confronting the middle-aged Frenchman who took major responsibility for the smooth running of the department.

'Is something the matter?' But his puzzled gaze was fixed not on her but on her companion.

So Dougal wasn't a spy. Clearly Delacroix countenanced his presence in the office.

'No, no really.' She hastened into speech intent on making her point. 'Dougal was enquiring about access to the Triple I file and I was just explaining I couldn't key him in because his name wasn't on the list of accredited personnel.'

It was the total deathly silence that followed this announcement that told her something was drastically wrong.

'Alex...' Delacroix regarded her flushed face, his expression a quaint mixture of shock and disbelief. 'Your devotion to the letter of regulations is admirable, but as a director of our parent bank in Paris, *Monsieur* du Gard...' he emphasised the courtesy title '...has automatic access to anything he chooses to inspect. That should have gone without saying.'

She was going to faint. Alex's lids dropped briefly over her blue eyes, as she fought to gain control of her emotions. Even if she'd heard his name correctly she wouldn't have associated it with the eminent Gallic financier of banking legend: the man who had graduated from *l'Ecole d'Administration* with the qualification of *Inspecteur des Finances* and turned down an offer to enter the Treasury, choosing instead the world of merchant banking and accepting a directorship of the Banque de Varcennes at the age of thirty.

She would have expected their renowned director to have been a much older man than the individual now regarding her with brooding dislike through thickly lashed, impatient eyes. But the damage had been done and she wouldn't compound her stupidity with stumbling explanations.

Drawing herself to her full five feet six inches, she inclined her head briefly. 'It seems I owe you an apology, Monsieur du Gard. Since you offered me no proof of your identity, I mistook you for someone else.'

'A dog, I believe you said?' He smiled unpleasantly. 'When you know me better you'll find my bite is twice as painful as my bark!' His dark eyes glittered with something which could have been amusement if only the set form of his sensuous mouth hadn't belied it. It was a look which promised her all kinds of future retribution. A look which warned her that the friendly ambience of her pleasant office was about to be shattered.

'Then I shall have to take care to avoid it, shan't I?' She forced herself to speak flippantly, determined not to let him see how weak she felt inside. Curse the VUO which had brought her to these depths! 'But I thought

my days here were numbered anyway?' Her sense of
humour rising to the surface, she couldn't stop the brief
smile which illuminated her face as she ran one finger
lightly across the front of her neck, as she challenged
his forbearance.

'You have two seconds left,' he answered gently, not
returning her smile and seemingly oblivious of Delacroix
who hovered in the background. 'Now will you key me
in, please, Alex?'

Having established his superiority, he addressed her
with condescending familiarity. She obeyed him, going
through the preliminaries with quick, practised fingers.
When the password was requested she filled in the four-
letter word with no hesitation. For security reasons it
did not print out on the screen, but du Gard's lustrous
eyes had missed nothing of her fingers' journey over the
keyboard.

'T.O.N.Y.,' he mused. 'Doubtless the name of the man
in your life?'

She shrugged, not denying it.

'You disappoint me, Alex. Far too obvious. Any fool
could crack it.'

'You didn't,' she said sweetly.

'But then I hadn't met you. I don't know details of
your—*amours*.'

'Not many people do.' She rose abruptly to her feet.
'You're in. Be my guest.'

'Thank you.' But he made no move to occupy the seat
she vacated, continuing to evaluate her with such a steady
appraisal that she became increasingly conscious of the
slight puffiness round her eyes, the pallidity of her
complexion and the cracked skin on her normally smooth
mouth, the legacies of the wretched VUO which had to
share some of the responsibility for her present uncomfortable situation.

In the background Delacroix was fussing around apologising on her behalf, singing her praises, explaining that she was one of the few non-French nationals employed in London because of her general aptitude and excellent command of the French language.

'Perhaps one can't always rely on first impressions, then.' Du Gard nodded sympathetically, obviously intent on making her pay for the sin of not knowing who he was.

The male ego at its most narcissistic. Alex sighed with heavy resignation. 'Do you wish to use my VDU or not, Monsieur du Gard? Because if you don't I've got a lot of work to catch up on.'

'And if I do?' His dark brows elevated.

'Then I shall go and make myself a coffee and sit in the staff lounge until I can get back to my desk!' she told him firmly.

'In that case I have a better idea. We'll both go up to the office I've appropriated on the next floor and work there.' He smiled, but his target was Delacroix, not her. 'I imagine that, since the department has run smoothly for the last week without Alex's presence, it can continue to do so for the next three weeks?'

'Now wait a moment,' she interposed hurriedly, seeing the vision of her normal pleasant working life shattered into fragments. 'I may not have recognised your eminence, but then you may not realise that I'm not part of a typing pool——'

'You do me an injustice!' White teeth gleamed for a moment as the tiger smiled. 'The invitation wouldn't have been extended to you if you had been. We're in the process of some extremely delicate negotiations, which is why I flew over from Paris last Thursday. Confidentiality is paramount. Unless I can trust someone absolutely, then I must work alone.'

'You're saying that you trust *me*?'

He expelled his breath impatiently. 'My dear Alex, I'm not extracting you from your cosy nest for the purposes of either pleasuring or punishing you—whatever you may believe! I need help and I've decided you are the person to provide it. You can start by arranging for a couple of VDUs to be installed in my office—and, when you get your own coffee, perhaps you'd be kind enough to bring one in for me.'

A quick nod of his sable head indicated the conversation was ended and he was striding out of the room.

It wasn't the way she would have chosen to start the week, but, always ready to face a challenge, Alex felt her pulse quicken in expectation as the adrenalin began to pump through her veins. So often the backroom girl in the bank's highly successful sorties, she was being given a ringside seat and, even though it carried the penalty of sharing business hours with the hostile director from France, she made up her mind to enjoy the experience as much as she could!

'Alex! You're late!' Simone jumped excitedly to her feet, her whole attitude one of suppressed excitement.

'Unavoidable, I'm afraid. The train I was on developed a faulty door and had to be taken out of service.' She glanced at her watch. 'Only fifteen minutes, though. What's up? Don't say someone's made a take-over bid for us, for a change?'

'No, it's Alain du Gard! He's back here again in a foul temper and demanding you go up to his office the moment you put in an appearance!'

'Is he indeed?' Unhurriedly Alex removed the tailored jacket of her newly made eau-de-Nil linen suit, hanging it in the wardrobe as Simone's gaze passed admiringly over her.

'That's a Louis Féraud copy, isn't it? I remember seeing it in *Elle*. Wow, Alex, I wish I had your talents with a sewing machine.'

'I'm pleased with it myself.' Alex accepted the other girl's praise graciously. 'It was so comparatively inexpensive to make that I treated myself to the silk blouse to add to the effect.'

'You look a million dollars,' Simone told her sincerely. 'But then you always do. Better not keep him waiting,' she added, the pleasure dying from her face. 'He really does look pretty mad.'

With an appearance of calm, Alex sat down at her desk. 'I'll just sort through these papers first.'

She saw, and ignored, the way Simone chewed at her lower lip. Unless Alain du Gard was in need of urgent heart resuscitation, a few more minutes couldn't be that vital. Besides, she needed to gather her wits together. For four weeks she and Alain had worked side by side and the experience had been everything she had expected—more, in fact.

Over the weeks her first impression that he was coolly arrogant, confident and remote in his own small world had changed as she had begun to perceive a hard-working man, living away from his friends and family, performing an intensive and demanding job. With this recognition had come greater tolerance, although the original tension which had sparked between them on that first meeting had never been entirely neutralised.

The day, two weeks earlier, when the City pages had been ablaze with the Triple I merger masterminded and funded by the Banque de Varcennes, and Alain had announced his plans to spend a short time in Bradford before returning to the Paris branch, she had felt both elated at the successful outcome of the venture and strangely depressed, as if she were losing something precious and irreplaceable.

Too many weeks had passed for her odd deflation to be attributable to post-viral infection. If she'd had time to analyse it she might have worked it through her system, she thought, but with Martine's urgent admission to hospital and Tony's need for her help and companionship she had thrust her own depression to the back of her mind. In fact, with the end of April bringing with it an unusual burst of spring sunshine, she had fancied her spirits had begun to lift again.

Clearly she had been fooling herself. Whatever the root of her *malaise*, Alain du Gard's unexpected return had triggered a relapse. Her pulse was beating a rapid beat, noticeable at her wrist and throat, and her entire body felt as if it had been put on 'yellow alert'. Absurd— when she had nothing to be apprehensive about!

She restacked the papers, having read not one word of anything, too immersed in the power of her own reactions to his unexpected reappearance to concentrate.

'Monsieur du Gard gave you no idea of why he's come back here?' she asked. Although he had continued to address her by her Christian name in the informal fashion adopted throughout the department by the clerical staff, she had constantly stayed with the formal style of address, initially embarrassed by her misunderstanding at their first meeting. If he had requested she address him as 'Alain' she might have done so. But the invitation had never been extended. That last day he had shaken her hand, thanked her for her help and wished her *bonne chance*! Damn the man for re-entering her orbit, when she was only just recovering from the effect of his previous disruptive presence!

Simone shrugged. 'The only impression I got was that he was deeply aggrieved by your absence, as if it were some personal insult!'

'Probably because he has no idea of the problems of travelling across London by Tube in the rush hour. It's about time someone told him we don't all have chauffeur-driven Jaguars at our command!'

'Or Lamborghinis!' Simone grinned at her. 'That was what you said you wanted, wasn't it?'

For a moment Alex was puzzled, then she remembered what she had jokingly said at the previous year's office party when she had been laughingly teased about her lack of a serious boyfriend.

'Oh, sure,' she agreed, her blue eyes gleaming with amusement as she repeated her attestation. 'No man will get me into church unless he can offer me a wedding dress by St Laurent, a honeymoon in St Lucia and a Lamborghini!'

'And what must a man offer you to get you into his office, half an hour after the first request was made, my dear Miss Hammond?'

There was no mistaking that voice. Alex looked round in dismay as Simone beat a hasty retreat across the office to enter Delacroix's partitioned-off sanctum. There was an edge to his voice and no trace of a smile on his granite-jawed face.

Silently cursing her ill-timed flippancy, Alex refused to apologise for it, choosing to meet his stony regard with wide-open innocent eyes. 'I wouldn't say no to a nice cup of coffee, Monsieur du Gard.'

She had hoped to defuse his antagonism, but in vain.

'Where the devil were you last night?' he demanded, his voice thick with annoyance.

Over the weeks they'd shared an office she'd grown accustomed to his detached coolness, his air of effortless superiority, but she'd never seen him quite so tensed and aggressive.

Biting back the indignant retort which rose to her lips, she paused, taking in his appearance with critical eyes. He was immaculately dressed as usual, this time in a slate-blue suit, but there were unaccustomed dark shadows under his golden eyes, the taut skin of his cleanly shaven face appearing pale and strained.

Was he not feeling well? she wondered. A hangover perhaps? But the clarity of his eyes behind the shield of dark lashes denied it. There seemed little point in provoking him further.

'Staying with a friend,' she told him honestly, her raised eyebrows tacitly demanding what business it was of his anyway.

'Hmm.' He managed to make the monosyllable sound scathing, as his brows met in an uncompromising line above his straight, assertive nose. 'You disappoint me. It seems that, not only do you know very little about the managerial structure of the company which employs you, but you're also unaware of the fact that key personnel are supposed to leave an address and phone number with the security department so they can be contacted in emergencies!'

Irritated as she was, Alex had to hide a smile at this quirk of vanity. So it still rankled that she hadn't immediately recognised him at their first meeting! Uncomfortably aware of the unaccountable aura of tension that constantly thrummed between them, she also knew this was no time to let him glimpse her amusement.

'I know the rule,' she returned mildly, her carefully modulated voice clear and clipped. 'What I didn't know was that I was classified as key personnel. Surely that honour falls to Monsieur Delacroix as head of the department?'

She watched his mouth harden, the strong curves thin to a harsh line as he told her heavily, 'Before I went to Bradford you were working for me. I assumed you'd realise that automatically made you key staff!'

'Quite frankly, Monsieur du Gard, from what I heard, from the first day you stepped over the threshold of this branch, *everyone* was working for you!'

Really, he was impossible! She flicked a stray tendril of blonde hair away from her cheeks as she observed the formidable glint of disfavour darkening the tawny eyes that pinned her attention. And to think that once, briefly, in the midst of worrying about Martine and caring for Tony, she had wondered if her sudden lack of vitality was due to the absence of mental stimulation she had been suffering in the wake of his departure!

'*D'accord.*' The agreement came smoothly, riding over her sarcasm as if it had never existed. 'So, please, in future make sure you can be contacted after hours.'

Resisting the impulse to salute smartly and say 'Yes, sir!' Alex decided against arousing his uncertain temper to greater effect, contenting herself with asking bleakly, 'Does the emergency still exist?'

'Emergency?' The cool amber regard of his frown suggested she was asking a riddle, then his expression cleared. 'Oh, that. No. After phoning you several times until the early hours of the morning, I decided the matter would have to wait until I could sort it out myself first thing this morning.'

'That's fine.' No way would she question him further. 'But you wanted to see me anyway?'

'Yes, yes, I did.' Having made his point, he seemed to relax slightly. 'There's been a change of plan. I was intending to return directly to Paris following my visit to Bradford, but the chairman has asked me to remain in London until further notice. Since our partnership

was so successful in pinning down the facts and figures
required for the Triple I merger ahead of our rivals, I've
asked Monsieur Delacroix to let me have your services
until further notice.'

Not again. Panic caught Alex unexpectedly in the
throat. Formless emotions she had refused to recognise
played havoc with her sympathetic nervous system,
making it difficult for her to breathe. Alain du Gard
threatened the simple equilibrium of her pleasantly
organised life. Instinctively she knew it.

It wasn't just his appearance. Sure, the typing pool
had been agog ever since he'd swum into their ambience,
and even Simone had endlessly detailed his physical perfection in his absence. She, herself, had never been impressed by appearance alone, although she had no
argument against the general consensus of female
opinion that Alain du Gard would not be out of place
on a male pin-up calendar.

It wasn't just the clear-cut lines of his face, she
admitted, or the thick smoothness of his hair and the
luminosity of his tigerlike eyes. Since working in close
proximity to him she knew his beautifully cut jackets
hadn't flattered the breadth of his shoulders, and his
equally elegantly tailored trousers hadn't required any
of the tailor's tricks to accentuate the hard, fluid lines
of mature masculinity at its breathtaking best.

It had been only natural that with her interest in dressmaking such details shouldn't have escaped her notice,
she told herself. But such things left her unmoved. No,
if she had to define it, then her reticence sprang from
an awareness of a feral spirit lurking behind the polished
exterior Alain du Gard presented to the world. She sensed
depths in him that were dark and dangerous. There was
no reason why they should affect her—yet the simple
unexplained knowledge of their existence seemed to be

a warning. Wasn't it said that coming events cast their shadows before them?

'Is something wrong, Alex?'

'No—only...do I have a choice?'

For ten seconds he studied her, making her uncomfortably aware of the rise and fall of her breasts beneath the pale green silk which faithfully followed their soft curves, then his eyes grew warm with amusement.

'No, I don't think so. You've already stated your terms, haven't you? If I'm prepared to meet them, I don't see how you can refuse me—unless you have another contender waiting in the wings—do you?'

His voice was smooth as satin, soft as velvet—and shook her to the core. For one mad instant she thought he was referring to her joke about the Lamborghini and took a half-step backwards away from him, her mind filled with images too chaotic to focus, then his voice, deeper this time and with a hint of impatience,

'Coffee, Alex. Coffee. That was what you said you wanted, wasn't it?'

CHAPTER TWO

ALEX had expected a busy morning, and so it proved.

'We're involved in very sensitive dealings in which both the French and British Governments have an interest, which is why the Banque de Varcennes is in an ideal position to offer advice,' Alain told her, handing over the promised coffee which, to her astonishment, he had made himself. 'What I need, Alex, is a full background on the companies listed in here.'

She watched his hands as he lifted a rigid briefcase on to his desk, twirling the security locks before producing a tightly packed manila folder. Beautifully manicured, strong yet sensitive hands, she noted, almost against her will. The hands of a man capable of tenderness and perception, though that was hardly the impression he generated, especially now when the vibes emanating from him were so coldly efficient.

Taking the proffered folder from him, she glanced at the contents, her mouth moving into the shape of a soundless whistle as she recognised some of the names involved, instantly appreciating the delicacy of the situation.

'I see you understand the implications.' He hadn't missed her quick reaction. 'Normally I would have dealt with this entirely by myself—in fact that is what the chairman believes I shall be doing, which is why he has asked me to stay on in London, but, since an urgent appraisal could mean the difference between a notable success for us and an ignominious withdrawal, I've decided to trust your discretion.' Golden eyes met and held her frank blue gaze. 'Based on your previous track record.'

'Thank you, I won't let you down.'

'That's what I'm counting on, Alex.' The smile he gave her then was open and generous. 'I'll be in and out of the office all day. Phone calls won't worry you because I'm having a secretary seconded to me, and she'll be intercepting all incoming calls, so you can devote all your time to the job in hand. I'm sure you know exactly what is wanted.'

Yes, she certainly did. Neither did she underestimate the scope of the task. By lunchtime the picture she required was gradually building and a pattern was evolving. It was similar to composing an enormous jigsaw and she found it equally absorbing, experiencing a real thrill of accomplishment when an unlikely source revealed a hidden directorship or movement of capital which hadn't been initially obvious.

Alain's protracted absences had proved something of a relief, she admitted, running a hand through her hair before rising to her feet and stretching her cramped body luxuriously. In his presence she always felt on edge, as if in some way he was holding her up for judgement and finding her wanting. Yet he had expressed his confidence in her without exception. She should have felt flattered. In truth she did! Why was it then that she still felt as if in some way she was falling beneath his expectations? And more to the point—why should she care?

Deciding to take a quick lunch, she locked up the results of her morning's endeavour, closed the computer file she had been accessing and made her way to a local sandwich bar, pleased to find Simone already there.

Refreshed after her break and the chance to relax with a friend, she paid a quick visit to the ladies' room to refresh her make-up and brush her soft blonde hair into shape, returning to the office to find Alain had returned.

'Ah, you're back,' he greeted her with raised eyebrows.

'So are you,' she observed silkily. 'Did you particularly want to see me?'

'You could say that.' To her discomfort he submitted her to a steady appraisal as his eyes drifted over the full length of her body.

'Is something wrong?' It was impossible for her to control the sudden flush of embarrassment which spread through her under his encompassing yet dispassionate gaze. Furious with herself because she hadn't blushed like that since she'd been an adolescent, she regarded him stonily.

'Not that I can see,' he responded smoothly. 'I was hoping you'd give me an update on your findings.'

'Of course.' She recovered the relevant papers, watching defensively as he studied them with no discernible expression on his personable face.

'Hmm. What are the chances of having full details today?' He laid the last sheet of print-out on his desk.

Alex shrugged her shoulders. 'It depends on what I uncover, but I'll do my best.'

'Good girl! What man could ask for more?' He glanced down at his watch. 'I have another appointment this afternoon, but I hope to be back by five. If I'm not just leave everything as far as you've got in the same place.' He nodded towards the drawer she had used previously. 'I have a duplicate key, and, Alex...'

'Yes?' She paused on the point of resuming her seat, taken aback as he came towards her, one hand touching her lightly on the shoulder as if he were bestowing an accolade, as he made for the door.

'Well done.'

By five o'clock the picture was nearly, but not quite finished. True to his forecast, Alain returned just as the minute hand of the clock moved towards the twelve.

To Alex's discerning eye he looked weary and she felt a small spasm of sympathy for him, aware of the responsibility he was shouldering and suddenly glad to be able to bear a part of it herself—even though her role would never be recognised officially.

To his query about her progress she added quietly, 'Would you like me to stay on for an hour or so and finish the whole report before the weekend?'

'Could you?' His face brightened immediately. 'That would give me over forty-eight hours' start to make a full assessment!'

She nodded, her own eagerness to complete the job making the offer no sacrifice. 'I'll have to make a phone call first.'

She would have to cancel the visit she'd intended to make to the hospital to see Martine, but her friend would understand, and as long as she told Tony she'd be late back so he didn't worry there'd be no problem. Her fingers punched out his number.

'Tony—it's me. Look, can you go on without me? I'm going to work later than I intended this evening, but I'll be there in time for dinner.'

She listened to his ready acceptance of her change of plans before replacing the receiver and removing the disk from the computer preparatory to replacing it with another one.

'So Tony's still the man of the moment?' Alain's voice at her shoulder caused her to swing round in surprise. He was regarding her with narrowed eyes and a slight sardonic lift of one dark eyebrow.

Immediately she bristled. Her personal life wasn't up for discussion and she resented the implication that she'd

be prepared to discuss it. If only he knew! An imp of
mischief made her slant him an amused glance. Determined as she was not to discuss Tony or his place in her
life with Alain or anyone else, he should have an answer
of sorts, and an honest one at that.

'Very much so,' she agreed demurely.

'You don't wear his ring!' Before she realised what he
intended to do, he'd reached out for her hand, taking
her fingers in his own. It was the second time that day
that he had touched her. This time as their bare flesh
met a shiver of anticipation ran through her, as, frighteningly aware of his body warmth communicating itself
to her, she pulled her hand away from his.

'No,' she returned, as calmly as she could, praying he
hadn't noticed how she'd trembled at the unexpected
contact. Expecting her agreement to end the conversation, she was unprepared when he continued to regard
her thoughtfully.

'Perhaps he can't offer you all the things you want in
life?'

There was a derisive note in his voice which jarred,
raising her antagonism.

'Too right he can't!' she agreed crisply, determined
that he wasn't going to get the explanation for which he
was angling. Not only was it none of his business, but
the facts were complicated and might portray Tony in a
poor light to someone as self-sufficient and authori-
tative as Alain du Gard.

'So you're "just good friends"?' he persisted,
regarding her with a slight smile twisting the corners of
his strong mouth. 'Isn't that how the media describe it?'

'I'm not interested in media descriptions any more than
I am in discussing my affairs, Monsieur du Gard!' There
was a touch of ice in her voice as she dismissed his

curiosity. 'If you want a result this evening, I'd appreciate your letting me have the last print-out I gave you.'

'*D'accord!*' He smiled without humour, placing the print-out on her desk. 'Your discretion is admirable, Miss Hammond.' He emphasised her formal name as if to reprove her for non co-operation. 'But then you wouldn't be working for me if it weren't, would you?'

He walked away, strolling to the window overlooking one of the narrow streets which formed the heart of London's busy financial centre, and staring down at the rush-hour traffic while Alex tried to collect her thoughts.

So it had been some kind of test, had it? He'd merely wanted to discover how easy it was to break through her defences. Well, she thought grimly, she'd passed that test with flying colours and she hoped he was as satisfied as his final announcement suggested. She bent her head and applied herself to her task.

Two hours later and it was finished.

After a cursory glance at the completed file, Alain du Gard laid it down on his desk.

'I'll buy you dinner,' he said abruptly. 'You've earned it.'

'But I already have a date,' Alex reminded him gently.

'Break it!' The command came with all the authority of his personality. 'You've already admitted your Tony can't give you what you want in life!'

'And you can?' She found his brooding contemplation so amusing that it was impossible to prevent the laughter that burst from her throat. 'I promise you I want more than an excellent dinner!'

'Oh, I'm quite aware of that, *ma chère* Alex,' he returned softly. 'I know how strongly St Laurent, St Lucia and a Lamborghini feature in your plans, but it's a little premature for me to be offering those.'

His sarcasm was like a slap round the face. Surely he didn't really believe that stupid joke? But two could play at that game.

'In which case Tony can offer me a great deal more than you can,' she told him sweetly. Let him think she meant material goods if he wanted to. Her own valuation was based on friendship, understanding and kindness. None of which attributes she had discerned in the irritating man whose presence had altered the even tenor of her life these last few weeks.

She walked to the wardrobe, and removed her jacket preparatory to leaving.

'Allow me.'

Before she could prevent it, Alain took the garment from her hand, holding it while she slid her arms into the soft lining.

'Am I allowed to compliment you on your dress sense?' he enquired drily, not allowing his hands to linger near her as he finished his task. 'St Laurent, is it?'

'Louis Féraud, actually. I've always favoured his day wear.' Let him make of that what he would.

His reaction left her in no doubt that her home dressmaking techniques had fooled him, she congratulated herself delightedly.

'I'm glad the bank pays you such an excellent salary. Obviously there's no need for me to put a word in for you at head office. Oh, and, Alex...before you go...' and as she tilted her head enquiringly ' ...just in case I need to contact you later in the evening—do I use the phone number on record?'

'No—no, I shan't be there.' She hesitated, uncomfortably aware that the question was not a sincere request in case he needed further information. The only information Alain du Gard wanted was to know where—and probably with whom—she intended to spend the night.

Why? They'd worked together for four weeks and, although the atmosphere between them had been charged with an indeterminable current—something like a reverse magnetism—he'd never shown such an interest in her private life before.

He'd gone out of her life—supposedly forever—and she'd missed him, the strange power he had possessed to charge her life with excitement and a tension which had been as enjoyable as it had been uncomfortable: something like taking a ride on a helter-skelter. Now he had returned and in one day she had registered a subtle difference in him. Now he was encroaching on areas of her life she wasn't prepared to share. Yet to refuse to answer him would only alienate him, making him even more difficult to work with.

He was waiting for her answer, pen poised over diary in hand. She gave him Tony's number, carefully keeping the resentment from her voice, adding for good measure, 'I'll be there all over the weekend.'

'Ah, yes,' he murmured, a note of cool perception colouring his deep tones. 'Of course.'

A few minutes later she sank gratefully on to the last available seat in the crowded Tube train, flashing a smile of gratitude to the middle-aged man who had stood aside to allow her access.

That was the acceptable face of male chauvinism, she told herself ruefully as she stared down at the cover of the glossy magazine she'd purchased at the station bookstall. Not like the reverse side of the coin from which she'd just escaped.

She didn't take kindly to coercion and domination. Why should she? She'd never been treated as anything but a responsible human being in her own right all the way through her business and personal life. Of course, she'd been lucky in having had a warm and secure home background, but she'd worked hard at school and had earned for herself the respect accorded to a capable employee.

Her eyes stared unseeingly at the cover of the magazine, not focusing on it. It was only natural she should feel resentment at Alain du Gard's condescending attitude towards her. What stimulus, she wondered, had provoked the polite indifference of the previous weeks to turn into the disquieting aggravation which had replaced it? Something had happened to alter the status quo—perhaps some incident which had occurred while he was in Bradford? Certainly nothing for which she could be indicted!

Dismissing the problem temporarily from her mind, she forced herself to concentrate on the periodical resting on her lap. It was nearly an hour later when she let herself into the pleasant semi-detached house only a mile away from her own apartment.

'Tony! Are you in?' She wrinkled her nose in an effort to detect the smell of the boeuf bourgignon she'd prepared the previous evening—and found nothing.

'I'm here, Alex!' Tony Gibson emerged from the kitchen, running long, sensitive fingers through his wheat-coloured hair. 'I was just lighting the gas in the oven,' he explained, a look of anxiety on his pleasant features. 'I think I left it a bit late, didn't I?'

'A little.' Alex laughed at his guilty expression. 'But don't worry. It's cooked already. It only needs reheating, and to be honest I've had such a hectic day my appetite seems to have disappeared.' She made her way into the attractive sitting-room with its view over a carefully cultivated garden, and subsided with a sigh on to one of the deep, comfortable armchairs, kicking her shoes off as she did so and curling her long, shapely legs beneath her. 'Oh—that feels a lot better!'

'Like that, is it?' Tony, who'd followed her, smiled sympathetically, gazing down at her with affectionate commiseration. 'I told Martine you weren't able to visit her tonight because the infamous Alain du Gard had made a priority call on your services.' He flung himself into the chair facing her own across the room. 'She gave me a message for you. Roughly translated it says—"That one's dynamite—treat with extreme caution!"'

'Really?' Alex blinked in surprise. It was a bit late now to receive such advice. 'I'd no idea Martine knew anything about him.'

'Ah, and there you'd be wrong.' Tony grinned wryly. 'I must admit it came as quite a surprise to me too, but she's surprisingly well informed—enough to write his biography, I reckon. It's a good job I'm not the jealous type.' He pulled a humorous face. 'I had to sit through most of the visiting time listening to her recollections of the illustrious Alain.'

Intrigued despite herself, Alex leaned forward. 'What did she say?'

Tony settled himself more comfortably, crossing his jeans-clad legs. 'Well, you remember she went back to Paris for three weeks on a training course the year before we got married? While she was there du Gard was appointed a director.' His face broke into a charming, boyish grin. 'My lovely wife described him as being "brilliant and beautiful" with a devoted following among the girls at the Paris branch, all of whom were destined to be disappointed because the president of the bank had a ravishing teenage daughter called Claudine who was being groomed to become Madame du Gard.'

Tony and Martine had been married for over three years—so Alain must be married. She'd always suspected he must be. It was hardly likely a man like Alain du Gard—mature, wealthy, handsome and successful—

would still be single, so why did she feel such a deep sense of disappointment? Probably because Simone had never mentioned a wife, and her friend had seemed to be singularly *au fait* with Alain's curriculum vitae. In any case, what concern was it of hers? He might have a wife and half a dozen children as far as she was concerned.

'What's the matter, Alex?' As Tony's voice penetrated her thoughts, she raised her eyes to find he was looking at her with a speculative gleam in his grey eyes. Her already disrupted equanimity wasn't restored when he added musingly, 'It seems to me that Martine's warning has come a little late, hm? You've gone and fallen for this guy, haven't you, Alex?'

'No, of course not!' She denied it vigorously, shocked by the intensity of her feelings and desperately searching her emotions to justify her disclaimer. 'He's handsome in a rather brooding way, and undeniably clever. Obviously he's wealthy, and I dare say some women may find him charming when he exerts himself. Unfortunately, all he does for me is rub me up the wrong way!'

'A very disturbing feeling, clearly.' Tony smiled at her ruefully. 'My dear Alex, you're forgetting I've known you for most of your twenty-four years. You don't share someone's childhood and teenage years without building some kind of rapport that carries into adulthood. The fact is you'll find it harder to fool yourself than to fool me. From where I'm sitting Monsieur du Gard isn't nearly so abhorrent to you as you'd like us both to believe.'

Alex sighed. 'You're wrong, Tony—as time will doubtless prove.' Whatever the truth about her feelings, and for the first time she was desperately unsure of them, one thing was clear: there was no way she would ever allow herself to fall in love with a married man—and if the impossible had happened unknowingly—and there was no way she was admitting it could have—then she would ruthlessly eliminate every scrap of feeling from her heart!

There must be some other way in which she could explain the mixed feelings she harboured for the irritating Frenchman. For the first time Tony's normal percipience of her reactions must be wrong! Generally he could read her like the proverbial book because, as he'd reminded her, she, her brother Jamie and Tony himself had been friends for as long as she could remember, sharing the joys and fortunes of the Hampshire countryside. She'd always regarded Tony as another brother: brilliant, erratic Tony whose skill as a graphic artist was at last bringing him success in the advertising world.

When Jamie had married Sara, it was Tony who'd been the natural choice for best man. Alex would never forget coming home from her year's stay in Paris for the occasion and seeing the change in him. He'd been smarter, more in control of himself, and he'd had his arm around the girl who'd brought about the metamorphosis—Martine St Clair.

Suddenly her own irritations seemed of little account as she leaned forward in her chair, her face serious. 'Is there any news of when Martine will be discharged from hospital?' she asked anxiously.

'Three or four days, they say.' Tony's whole face lit up with pleasure. 'And, Alex, there's something else— the most marvellous news. Her consultant believes he can operate to help her. It seems there's a new technique that may correct the fault that makes her keep miscarrying.'

'Tony darling!' She was on her feet, eyes glowing with happiness as she perched on the arm of his chair, bending down to kiss his cheek. 'That's fantastic!'

As his arms came round her in a friendly hug she recalled the distressing occasions when Martine had lost her longed-for baby. Three times in as many years. Not only had they been traumatic experiences in themselves for the lovely French girl who'd become as close as a sister to her, but the effect on Tony had been devastating.

Not the most stable person at the best of times, he'd gone completely to pieces the first time Martine had been rushed to hospital. In fact he'd made himself so ill with self-imposed guilt that Martine had discharged herself well before she was fit.

The second time she'd lost the baby she was expecting Alex had acted quickly, to avoid a repetition. With the grateful consent of both parties she'd moved into the spare room in their house and taken Tony under her wing. It hadn't been just the matter of providing meals although, heaven knew, he'd probably have starved himself without supervision; it was the emotional support she'd been able to provide that had been so valuable.

In the early hours of the morning when Tony had been pacing the floors castigating himself as a monster, it had been Alex who'd talked to him, listened to him, made him cup after cup of tea and brought him back to a rational frame of mind.

Yes, she thought, with a wry, introverted smile, Tony was very much the 'man of the moment' in her life, although not in the way Alain du Gard had inferred! Although she'd been delighted to find on this last occasion of tragedy, that Tony's reactions had been much improved. The shy, clever young boy with whom she'd shared her childhood was at last maturing at the age of twenty-seven. Not before time, some people would condemn him unfeelingly, but then Tony was an artist and a superb one at that. Controlled by his temperament, he'd made every effort not to become a slave to it—and Alex was prepared to admire him for that! Besides, friendship, true friendship, had its obligations and ones she would always be prepared to fulfil.

Almost as if he could read her thoughts, Tony gave her his slow, sweet smile. 'Martine and I can never repay the debt we owe you, Alex,' he told her simply, and as she shook her head, rejecting all need for gratitude, he continued cheerfully, 'At least we've agreed you won't have to "baby-sit" with me next time. Martine has decided to invite her mother over from Lyons when she undergoes the operation that's been suggested to her— so I'll have someone else to hold my hand.'

There was a certain amount of shame in the statement which Alex moved quickly to stem. 'You've been a bit of a fraud this time,' she told him with a grin. 'You didn't need anyone to hold your hand—just cook your dinner! As a matter of fact, I'm so disgusted with your rude health and obvious capabilities that I intend to go back to my own place after the weekend!'

'You've seen through my bluff!' He laughed in mock dismay. 'Well, I guess I can cope for myself for the next few days before Marty gets back. Especially if you leave the fridge well stocked.'

'Splendid!' She gave him a stern look. 'Because my flat has been terribly neglected while I've been devoting myself to your culinary needs. I'll have to give it a good going-over when I get back there—provided the irresistible Monsieur du Gard doesn't find some other task to keep my nose to the grindstone each and every hour!' Her blue eyes sparkled as Tony chuckled delightedly.

'Sweet Alex—is he really such a tyrant? I don't think I've seen you look so outraged since you found out Andy had been two-timing you,' he teased.

Alex grimaced, letting the reference to Andy Charleson pass without comment. Neither Tony nor Martine had been impressed with the small-town solicitor she'd seen only at weekends when she returned to Hampshire to visit her parents, and, although they'd commiserated with her six months earlier when Andy had professed himself head-over-heals in love with a Titian-haired cabaret artiste, they'd both maintained she was worthy of a partner of a fierier steel.

Alain du Gard was certainly that, she admitted silently. Cool, clean steel. Hard and functional on the surface, with no clue as to what lay beneath the bright, shiny exterior.

'Alain du Gard gets under my skin,' she admitted to Tony. 'Though to be fair he's entitled to a certain amount of arrogance. He must have worked incredibly hard to graduate from *l'Ecole d'Administration* as young as he did with the qualifications of *Inspecteur des Finances*.' She shrugged slim shoulders. 'So, as a banker, he deserves admiration.'

'But not as a man?'

This was dangerous ground and Alex wasn't ready to commit herself, even to one of her oldest friends.

'I don't really know him as a man,' she prevaricated, rising to her feet quickly before Tony could taunt her further about feelings she had no wish to analyse. 'I bet you forgot to put the potatoes on!' she scolded, glad of an opportunity to leave the room and end the conversation.

Behind her she heard Tony's laughter.

'Something which I have a feeling is soon to be remedied!' he called after her.

Of course he was referring to the potatoes... but why should that cause a shiver of premonition to run down her spine? she wondered, and refused to waste precious leisure time searching for an answer.

CHAPTER THREE

'DAY-DREAMING, Alex?'

'Certainly not!' she denied the suggestion vigorously, despite the fact that Alain's previously undetected arrival in the office suggested otherwise. 'As a matter of fact I was just thinking that, now you've completed your report and the preliminary meetings, there's not much point in my continuing to share your office. I really should be going downstairs and getting on with my own work. Poor Monsieur Delacroix and Simone have been carrying an extra workload ever since you came back!'

'A fact of which I'm not unaware.' He met her frank gaze with contemplative eyes, bright behind the shield of dark lashes. 'Has it been so unpleasant working with me, then, Alex?'

'No, of course not.' Her mouth was unexpectedly dry. Even if that had been the case she would never have been so uncivil as to put it so bluntly, but the opposite had been true. Two weeks had passed since his return from Bradford and he had demanded her exclusive services.

She'd originally supposed that, her having supplied him with the details he'd requested on that first day, he would no longer wish her to remain in the same office. Instead he'd insisted on her continuing presence, even taking her with him to two highly confidential meetings outside the bank, where he'd introduced her as his assistant.

'I feel I'm being accepted under false pretensions,' she'd protested after the first occurrence. 'Really,

Monsieur du Gard, although I appreciate your trust, I'm only basically a researcher.'

'On the contrary, you're whatever I choose to make you,' he'd told her peremptorily. 'And at the present time I choose to have you as my assistant.'

'But——' she'd begun to protest, her normal confidence shaken by the greatness to which he had elevated her at such short notice.

'No "buts", Alex!' he'd interrupted her briskly. 'Not only do you have brains but you have style and beauty too. At this moment you fill a place in the scheme of things. If you disappoint me—be sure I'll let you know.'

She had had to be satisfied with that, shrugging her shoulders resignedly.

'If it's extra remuneration for the responsibility that concerns you,' he'd added harshly, 'you can rest assured that I shall personally see you are adequately reimbursed!'

It hadn't been her concern, and she was wounded that he should even suspect it, but he hadn't waited for her response, effectively blocking any reply she might have made by picking up his phone and punching out a number.

So their uneasy relationship had continued: smooth and jagged by turn, frustrating at times, but always exhilarating, even when she was silently cursing him for some unreasonable demand, but the time had come for it to finish. She knew it in her heart. Now that the work he'd been brought back to finish was completed and only the result awaited, he would soon be returning to Paris. Deep inside herself Alex knew that, the sooner she made the break from him, the better it would be.

'No, of course not,' she repeated her denial, uncomfortably aware of his querulous look and raised eyebrows. 'In fact it's been a very stimulating experience and I'm grateful for the opportunity to enjoy it, but it's over as far as I'm concerned—so...' She waved her hand over her desk. 'As I said, as soon as I've cleared up these last bits and pieces I'll be going back to my own department.'

'That's hardly your decision to make.' His gentle reply belied both the formidable stance of his body and the frown which marred the classic bones of his face. 'We'll discuss the future plans I have for you over lunch.' A quick glance at his watch confirmed the time. 'Now will be as good a time as any.'

'I'd planned to have a sandwich,' she demurred. 'In fact I was just going to send out for one...' The hand she reached towards the buzzer which would summon a messenger boy was halted by a strong hand clasped round her wrist before she could execute her intention.

'I think not,' Alain murmured. 'A sandwich is no substitute for a well-balanced meal. I have a much better idea. I belong to a small club a few minutes' walk from here. There's a dining-room for members and their guests. Strictly table d'hôte, I'm afraid, but I've already checked the menu and if you like melon, fresh salmon salad followed by strawberries and cream, I'd be delighted to escort you there as my guest.'

It was a tempting offer. Alex could feel her mouth watering at the prospect, but the last thing she wanted to do was to enjoy his company socially. Every instinct for self-preservation reared up inside her.

'I really do prefer a sandwich,' she lied.

'And I prefer you don't have one!' He still held her wrist captive as their eyes clashed in battle, and she felt the dominating power of his will pierce her resolve. 'The service is fast, the break will do you good, the food is excellent—and, as I've said, I want to talk to you.'

'I'm sorry...' She used her free hand in an effort to loosen his restraining grip, feeling her pulse quicken as the movement brought her into an even more intimate contact with him, and she became vitally and disturbingly aware of the bitter-sweet tang of aftershave and the warmth radiating from his clear skin.

'Besides which,' he continued pleasantly, waving aside her embryo protest and seemingly unaware of her reaction to his proximity, 'I haven't eaten since lunchtime yesterday and I've no appetite for a solitary meal.'

The pressure on her wrist vanished and she was able to lift it easily from his relaxed grasp. For a moment she remained transfixed, her own fingers encircling Alain's wrist, feeling the fast, steady beat of his pulse against their soft tips. Then, shocked by the unexpected thrill of pleasure the intimacy gave her, quickly she withdrew her hand, hoping that if he saw the flush of colour on her face he'd attribute it to anger rather than the heady confusion which now engulfed her.

He was still quite close to her: tall and very still, his dark head poised a little to one side, the flicker of a smile teasing the corners of his mouth, as amusement replaced Alex's original annoyance as she acknowledged the persuasive power in his change of tactics.

She couldn't deny that eating alone in a public place could be quite the opposite of relaxing, although she was astonished he should confess his preference for company—any company presumably, since she could hardly imagine she would be his natural first choice.

For the first time she considered accepting the invitation. She'd worked unflaggingly for the past two weeks and she deserved a treat! Just as long as he didn't think he'd cowed her into acceptance! Her mind made up, a small imp of mischief warmed the smile she turned on him.

'Since you appeal to my compassion rather than issue me with an order, I have to admit that fresh salmon is one of my weaknesses.'

'Then I couldn't be happier.' He made no effort to hide the gleam of triumph that sparkled in his eyes at her capitulation. 'Shall we go?'

'So you know Paris well?'

His tone was politely conversational as he refilled her wine glass with the dry, delicately scented Chablis Premier Cru, which he'd chosen to complement the delicious poached salmon they'd both enjoyed. The crisp, fresh taste of the wine had been so refreshing to her palate she'd declined his offer of a dessert wine to accompany the strawberries. Besides, she needed to keep a clear head.

'I like to think so,' she answered lightly, chasing the last strawberry round the silver bowl in front of her. 'And not just the tourist part either.'

How glad she was now she'd chosen to wear her Louis Féraud copy again, for the club to which he'd taken her was rather special, being situated on the second floor of one of the old London buildings which had escaped the City blitz of the 1940s. Sandwiched between two modern edifices, the old structure had eluded her attention until now. Glancing around, she knew she'd never have guessed that within its rather dour outer walls such a discreet, opulent haven might exist.

Thick burgundy-coloured carpet and heavy matching velvet curtains at the tall windows lent an air of luxury and warmth echoed by the polished mahogany panels of the walls, while the recessed lighting in the ceiling augmented the spring sunlight without adding glare.

Counting the tables as she'd entered, Alex had enumerated only ten in the dining area which also included a long and amply stocked bar. Now six of these with their snowy damask cloths, silver tableware and lead crystal glasses were occupied, a low buzz of conversation making a pleasant background murmur.

It was against this relaxing setting that Alain had gently prompted her about her commercial past. Not surprising really, as it was quite rare for a foreign branch of such an élite organisation as the Merchant Banque de Varcennes to employ anyone but their own nationals. Naturally he would wonder about her credentials, and since they were doubtless on record somewhere she had no qualms about informing him.

So between courses she'd told him about Madame Thierry and some of the things she'd enjoyed most about the French capital, explaining how it had been her language master at the private school she'd attended who'd suggested to her parents that their only daughter, after obtaining excellent A Level results, should spend a year on an exchange visit to Paris to perfect an accent which was already good and improve a fluency which was remarkable for a non-French national.

It had been a happy year, and at eighteen Alex had been grateful that her parents had been wealthy enough to sponsor her financially, and for the love and support they'd given her.

Not only had she won her independence in Paris, staying with the Thierry family, but her horizons had broadened. She'd fallen in love with the 'City of Light', entranced by the art exhibitions on the Ile de la Cité, fascinated by the stunning impact of Notre Dame and Sacré Coeur, intrigued by the village atmosphere of Montmartre.

It was in Paris she'd stared with envy at the beautiful fashion garments in the smart city shops a world away from the quiet Hampshire village of her birth and had discovered her own talent for dressmaking, taking lessons from the charming lady who'd opened her heart and home to the shy blonde English girl with her coltish figure and open affection for all things French—although Alex had spared the dark-browed man across the table from her such trivial personal information.

She was smiling softly at her own recollections when Alain asked diffidently, 'Did you never consider prolonging your visit?'

'For a while, yes.' She stopped speaking to take a sip of wine, allowing her mind to linger on the events of four years ago. 'Then my brother Jamie announced his wedding plans and I came back to England. As chance would have it, at the wedding I met his best man's fiancée. Martine's French and she was working here at the bank.' Replacing her glass on the table, she made a small gesture with her hands. 'I guess it must have been fate. There was an instant rapport between us and it was Martine who persuaded me to apply for a job in the same department. On the spur of the moment I agreed— knowing it would be an excellent opportunity to use my French. I imagine it was her recommendation that made the decision go in my favour.'

'That and your obvious abilities.'

Was he being sarcastic? Alex's sharp glance raked his austere face, but there was no glint of derision in his shadowed eyes as eloquent eyebrows lifted questioningly. 'Coffee?'

'Please.' She dipped her fair head in acquiescence, adding to the waiter who hovered over her, 'Black, please.'

'And for me.' Alain indicated his own cup.

'But your parents live in Hampshire, I believe you said?' Politely declining her offer of the chased silver sugar bowl, he referred to an earlier part of their

conversation. 'Since the telephone number you registered with Security is a London one, I assume you're
not a long-distance commuter?'

'Hardly.' Laughter sparkled in her blue eyes as she
met his polite curiosity. 'As a matter of fact the family
house has been let out for two years while my parents
are in Canada with my brother Jamie and his family.'

There was no need for her to say more, but the seemingly genuine interest of the man across the table from
her prompted her to a fuller explanation. 'When my
father retired as a general practitioner last year he and
my mother accepted my brother's invitation to visit him.
Jamie's a doctor, too,' she added, sparing a fond thought
for her elder brother and feeling a pang of regret that
it had been so long since she'd last seen him. 'In any
case,' she continued brightly, 'I was very lucky because
Martine was already living in a one-room flatlet in
London, so we pooled our resources and took a small
flat in Wimbledon as soon as I started working in
London nearly five years ago—until she got married.'

'And now you live there alone?' He was studying her
with a quizzical interest.

A vague feeling of disquiet invaded her, engendering
a sense of wariness in response to the gentle enquiry.
Why would Alain be interested in her domestic arrangements? she wondered. Perhaps he thought the bank was
overpaying her if she could afford to stay on alone after
Martine's departure! Still, she was under no obligation
to reveal every facet of her life, was she?

Quickly she decided against telling him that until three
months ago she'd been sharing with an old schoolfriend
who worked for a fashion company. It had been
fortunate that when Lindy had been temporarily seconded to New York the British branch of the company
had agreed to pay her share of the rent of the London

flat pending her return, but it was none of Alain du Gard's business! Despite his apparent interest, there had to be a limit to his fascination about her personal circumstances!

'For the time being—yes.' She looked at her watch. Good grief! She'd been away from the office for two hours. 'I'd no idea it was so late!' She put her dismay into words. 'I'll have to go!'

'Not yet!' It was a command that stopped her in the act of rising to her feet. Whether it was true or not that Alain hadn't eaten for twenty-four hours she couldn't decide, frowning slightly at his dictatorial tone, but he certainly looked better now than he had earlier in the day. It would be flattering to believe that her presence had been partly responsible for his recovery, but there was something now in his attitude that belied that assumption. 'If you remember, I told you I wanted to talk to you.'

'But we've been talking for two hours...' Confusion caused her to hesitate. She'd been talking—but then only at his instigation. Flushing a little, she resumed her seat. 'About business, you mean?'

'Correct. To be specific, about the job I have for you tomorrow at Epsom.'

'Epsom?' Puzzlement mantled her face. 'There's no branch of the bank there.'

'Correct again.' Amusement discovered and deepened elongated grooves at each side of his mouth. 'But there is a racecourse.'

'Well, naturally there is,' she returned a little sharply. 'It's where the Derby and the Oaks are run, but I fail to see what that has to do with me.'

'Then I shall explain.' He raised a peremptory finger demanding more coffee, waiting until both their cups had been refilled before continuing easily, 'As you may or may not know two thirds of the Banque de Varcennes is owned by the parent company in France. The remaining third is British-owned. The chairman of the insurance company which controls the British interest is also a personal friend of mine. It so happens I need to talk to him urgently and confidentially. Since he's a racing fanatic I've invited him to join me in the bank's private box at Epsom tomorrow. Fortunately even though it's not the Derby meeting there's still a very good card.'

'But what has that to do with me?' Alex demanded in genuine surprise.

'It's quite simple.' Did she detect a flicker of challenge in the golden, enigmatic eyes that surveyed her judiciously? 'Dudley's wife loves racing and she'll be coming down from Yorkshire with him. I'd hate to see her neglected, so I want you to entertain her while Dudley and I talk business.' He paused before adding, 'Liz is a charming lady—you'll like her.'

Looking askance at the handsome face across the table from her, Alex wasn't at all sure she cared for the assumption she would automatically agree to his plans when they fell so much outside the normal course of her duties. Neither, she determined, was she going to allow herself to be bribed by the meal he'd just bought her.

'Of course, I'm flattered by your confidence in my social graces, Monsieur du Gard,' her sweet smile had a touch of acid behind it, 'but I'm afraid I'm not interested in racing.' A tingle of anticipation quickened through her nerve cells as she opposed him.

'There's no requirement that you should be, my dear Alex.' The challenge deepened. 'The fact remains that I need a companion to facilitate my urgent discussions— and I've decided you are the ideal person.'

'Indeed?' A thought occurred to her and was put into words before she'd considered its advisability. 'I suppose if you were back in France you'd take your wife with you to entertain Mrs Moorhead?'

'My wife—or my mistress.' His agreement came silkily as he watched the soft tide of colour wash her fair skin, before he added softly, 'That is, if I possessed either— which at the moment I don't. Since I've been resident in England for such a short time, my choice of a suitable lady here is limited.'

So he wasn't married after all! What had happened to the delectable Claudine? she wondered briefly, feeling illogically as if she were on trial and resenting it. 'Otherwise you would hardly have asked me!' she remarked acidly.

To her chagrin he didn't deny it, continuing coolly, as he signed the bill which had just been presented to him, as if her remark was of no significance, 'In the circumstances I'd like Dudley and Liz to believe you and I are personal friends rather than mere business acquaintances.'

Alex stared back at his personable face as he replaced his gold Parker in an inside pocket of his expensive suit. Now it was clear that the lunch had been an audition to see if she met his stringent requirements for a temporary girlfriend!

The trouble with Alain du Gard was, she determined grimly, he was much too good-looking for his own good. The kind of man who normally had a bevy of girlfriends at his beck and call. He'd denied having a wife and— quite unnecessarily in her opinion—a mistress either, which still left a great number of indefinable relationships with women open to him, and she'd little doubt he'd sampled quite a few of them to date. How unfortunate that none of his present *involvements* was the right side of the Channel!

'Presumably,' she said between gritted teeth as she rediscovered her breath, 'it wouldn't do for your illustrious friends to know you were reduced to taking one of your own employees out with you on a social occasion!'

'I felt sure you'd understand the situation.'

His smooth agreement did nothing to assuage her feelings of being put on trial and then used. What a snob the man was! If he thought she was going to pretend to be anything other than she was, she had news for him.

'Don't worry.' There was amusement in his voice, as his quick eyes perceived the tightening of her jaw, the accent nearly perfect, only the slightly thickened burr of the 'r's suggesting his origin as south of the English Channel. 'I'm sure you can play the part to perfection.'

He really was the limit! Did he actually think her silence had been due to feelings of inadequacy? Swallowing down an angry retort, Alex made a determined effort to conceal her rising displeasure. Losing her temper would gain her nothing. There was a better way of demonstrating her displeasure.

'Thank you for your reassurance.' Her smile was honeyed. 'However, the question of my capabilities won't arise since I prefer not to accept your invitation.'

She rose swiftly to her feet, determined this time to leave, but Alain was too quick for her.

'It wasn't an invitation, *ma chère*.' He too rose to his full height, detaining her with a firm hand beneath her elbow. 'It was an instruction.'

'I'm sorry, Monsieur du Gard,' she responded tightly, pointedly ignoring his ironic endearment, 'but I'm employed by the bank to work at their City branch, not to follow the sport of kings!'

'You're wrong, Alex.' The contradiction came softly and fast, her given name sliding softly off his tongue as if it were an endearment. 'Look at your contract and you'll find you're employed in the bank's service to do as instructed by the management—provided it's in the line of duty, naturally.' A flicker of humour deepened the colour of his eyes to deepest oloroso.

'And going to Epsom is?'

'In these circumstances—most definitely.' The hand beneath her elbow tightened, demanding she change her decision.

'And if I choose not to go?' she asked, scorn lending a sharp edge to her normally soft voice.

'Then I'd assume you no longer wished to work for the Banque de Varcennes.'

Shocked disbelief froze Alex to the spot. It was incredible, but there was little doubt the threat was real. Alain du Gard—*financier extraordinaire*—was not to be defied with impunity. She'd already caught a glimpse of the harsh arrogance that lay beneath the veneer of good manners during the past weeks of working with him. Of course, she knew that if he carried out his threat she could take him to a tribunal. And *he* knew she had far too much pride to contemplate doing any such thing.

She drew in a deep breath to steady her temper. In this case discretion was certainly the better part of valour. What was the point of throwing up a job she enjoyed in order to make a point with a man whose conceit she despised? Besides, she wasn't without humour, and she might be able to find some compensatory amusement in the situation...

'Well?' He shot the question at her, his face unreadable.

Alex forced herself to dimple a smile at him. 'Suddenly I find the idea of a day at the races most attractive.'

'*Très bien*!' There was no denying the triumph in his reply as his hold slackened to a gentle guidance, edging her towards the exit.

'I'm touched by your faith in my capabilities!'

'Oh, indeed I have great faith in them,' he confirmed smoothly. 'In fact I'm relying on your past record to ensure the small deception I'm asking you to practise tomorrow goes off faultlessly.'

Professional blackmail, Alex thought wearily, recognising that if she had intended to embarrass him deliberately that course of action was now precluded. On the other hand, there were ways she could still make him uncomfortable...

'Of course, now I've accepted the exalted post you've offered me I'll do my best to carry it off,' she assured him, 'but you'll have to help me.' Gazing at him limpidly as outside in the narrow corridor they waited for the lift, she kept her expression exquisitely innocent. 'For instance—how would you expect a personal friend to address you? I can hardly call you *Monsieur le Directeur*, can I?'

Holding the assumed simplicity of her regard, unable to prevent a tell-tale muscle from twitching at the corner of his strong mouth as he detected but decided to ignore her irony, he retorted amiably enough, 'You're perfectly aware of my name, Alex—naturally you'll call me "Alain".'

'Alain.' She repeated the name as if she'd had no previous knowledge of its existence, breathing a depth of emotion into it that was a pole away from her true feelings at that moment. 'Very pretty—I like it.'

She put her head on one side, allowing the gleaming blonde hair to swing across her cheek. Since he wasn't married she felt able to tease him a little—subject him to some of the irritation he had inflicted on her! 'Or how about—Alain, *chèri*?' she enquired guilelessly, beginning to enjoy herself as his eyes narrowed in conjecture. 'Or would that be *too* personal for you?'

'Not at all. You may be as personal as you wish—outside the bank.' The suave reply came with the speed of a ricochet, as Alex dragged her eyes away from the firm lips which seemed to be having difficulty in keeping straight.

'Why, thank you!' Sarcasm made her voice tremble. 'And this delightful "personal" relationship of ours—suppose I forget myself and continue it after tomorrow?'

She'd hoped to annoy him. What she hadn't anticipated was the gleam of laughter that made the amber eyes glow with devilment, or the sudden flashing smile that incredibly caught at her heart-strings.

'I'm not usually interested in short-term contracts, but...' His pause was deliberately provocative as he let his gaze drift lazily over her lovely, defiant face. 'You're a singularly attractive woman in all senses of the word, as I'm sure you know. Make me a proposition by all means, Alex, and I promise to consider it.'

'Why, you——' Anger darkened the faultless azure of her furious eyes. But she'd made the challenge and she should have expected him to respond to it. Beneath the cold façade she now realised there lurked a highly dangerous male animal. Stripped of his authority and intellectual and social pretension, Alain du Gard was one hundred per cent predator—and the knowledge was oddly shocking.

Involuntarily she shivered at his gentle taunt, for the first time prepared to admit that the abrasive tension she'd sensed between them in the previous weeks could have its roots in sexual chemistry. Instinctively she now knew any game played with the man at her side would be fiery and furious. And everyone knew that those who played with fire got their fingers burnt!

Unconsciously she stretched out one of her slender hands in front of her, hardly seeing the smooth, well-cared-for skin or the oval, unpolished nails as she heard the sound of the approaching lift and let out a small sigh of relief.

'Don't worry.' She looked up into his face, her features taut with purpose as he stood aside to allow her to enter the conveyance first. 'That's one decision you won't be asked to make!'

Determined not to let her wayward thoughts and emotions disturb the smooth pattern of her work, she continued finalising it with renewed diligence, having regained the sanctuary of her office. After all, why let Alain's suggestion throw her? If he wanted to pretend a personal relationship existed between them, he could. Like Cinderella's, her masquerade would end promptly—and in her case long before midnight!

CHAPTER FOUR

'RIGHT!' Alex removed the disk from her computer and switched it off. 'That just about finishes everything.' The clock showed a few minutes past five o'clock as she collated the last few sheets of print-out and filed them neatly in the drawer of her desk, before turning to face Alain.

Although he'd been in the office the entire afternoon, he'd made no effort to speak to her or interfere with what she was doing. Unfortunately the quietness he'd observed had done nothing to make her oblivious of his presence, and she would be glad when she could escape the build-up of static tension which always seemed to occur when they shared an office.

She addressed him directly as he put down the magazine he'd been glancing at to meet her cool gaze. 'If there's nothing else you want from me, I'll be on my way home.'

'Oh, but there is something else...' He pushed his chair back, rising lazily to his feet as she paused in the doorway. 'When we were having lunch together you asked for my help in playing your part tomorrow—remember?'

He walked towards her as she stood hesitating, moving so close to her that she could discern the scent of his aftershave making a sharp and dangerous assault on her senses. His voice was low and husky, frighteningly beguiling as she opened her mouth to deny his allegation, despite the fact that her memory told her it was true.

Before she could utter a word he had captured her
shoulders with a light touch and was bending his head
towards her upturned face. She drew in a breath half
shocked, half outraged as his mouth skimmed hers,
gently brushing her parted lips.

The next moment awareness was flaming through her
with the stinging shock of an electric current, leaving
her helpless in its trail. In some dark corner of her mind
she knew she should protest, but her body was betraying
her, sighing its pleasure as it warmed to the sensual
caress. Immediately, as if he'd been waiting for her
signal, Alain sensed her response, sliding his arms round
her shoulders, drawing her closer to him, changing the
tempo of the embrace, turning what had been light and
flirtatious into something far more perilous. His mouth
hardened against her lips so that they parted against the
pressure, and she could feel the palms of his hands warm
and urgent against the thin linen that covered her back.

Sensation flooding through her, lifting her to a pitch
of excitement she'd never felt before in any man's arms,
Alex fought to regain her self-control, sensing that one
sign of further encouragement from her and Alain would
try to take her down a road she had no wish to travel.
Frantically, the adrenalin charging through her veins, she
pushed herself away, praying he hadn't detected the hard
swell of her breasts as they'd brushed his elegantly suited
chest. It was a prayer destined not to be answered, she
realised with a spasm of despair, as she evaluated the
slumbrous warmth of his golden eyes.

'Well, well . . .' To her relief he let her go, an odd little
smile playing round his mouth. 'I do believe you're not
going to find it too hard at all playing the part I asked
of you. Still—a rehearsal is never wasted.'

She swallowed hard, angry that he appeared so untouched while her own heart was thudding with as much

power as if she'd run a marathon. It might have been just a rehearsal for a fraud as far as he was concerned, but suppose she'd responded with more fervour? Suppose she'd dragged her fingers through his thick dark hair, offered the secrets of her mouth to his questing tongue, pressed her warm curves against him... Would he still be standing there so calm and superior—so totally unmoved?

Shocked by the passage of her thoughts, she forced herself to remain calm.

'I'm delighted you found my performance satisfactory, particularly as I hadn't expected being asked to provide one tonight! Now the rehearsal's over I assume I'm free to go home?' she asked coldly, hoping the icy crystals in her tone would convey her displeasure at his action, and that the quiver in her voice would be ascribed to temper rather than the result of shattered emotions.

'Of course.' He nodded as if nothing extraordinary had taken place between them. 'I found your spontaneity very rewarding.' He cast her a brooding glance. 'Take tomorrow morning off and make yourself beautiful. I want to be proud of you when I introduce you to my friends. I'll pick you up at your flat at twelve-thirty and we'll be meeting Dudley and Liz on the course in time for lunch in the grandstand restaurant before the meeting begins.' He paused delicately before adding, 'Unless of course you'll be spending the night somewhere else?'

'My own flat will be fine,' she confirmed crisply, resenting his sexist instructions, but deciding not to dignify them by direct reference. 'Do I need to bring anything with me?'

'Just a civil tongue,' he reproved her disdainful tone, irritating her further by showing no remorse for his condescension. 'A soft voice and a sweet smile. See what you can do.'

'*D'accord*, Monsieur du Gard!' The retort came smartly as she moved out of his range, not quite speedily enough. One large stride and he'd caught up with her, taking her by the arm and turning her round to face him.

'Alain,' he said, unsmiling. 'Remember? My name's Alain.'

Mutely she stared back at him, the pressure holding her rigid emanating from his eyes rather than his hands.

'Say it, Alex,' he commanded softly.

There was nothing he could do to her, nothing he *dared* do to her, but something about his intransigent stance, the cool glitter of the oloroso eyes, warned her to exercise caution.

'Alain,' she murmured obediently, refusing to look at him.

He released her instantly and she sped for the door, turning on the threshold, meeting his gaze and holding it. Was it really possible to feel such mixed emotions about a man? A confused medley of liking and detesting and—most frightening of all—desiring?

Pausing, she made a great show of fluttering her long eyelashes before forcing her mouth into a deliberately seductive smile, then dropped him a mock curtsy, her fair head bowed to him in assumed deference.

'Alain, *chéri*!' she amended sarcastically before walking quickly through the doorway, obeying the maxim that discretion was the better part of valour as she left the bank's premises with a brisk stride.

The following morning she whipped through the housework with efficient energy before relaxing in a hot bath. It was extra pleasant soaking in the perfumed bubbles knowing that she wasn't being sybaritic—merely dutiful. Alain wanted a glamour girl—and that was exactly what he was going to get, she thought determinedly.

Squeezing the sponge over her gleaming opaline breasts, she shivered despite the warmth of the water. What had possessed her to melt in his embrace as she had done? Tiredness alone couldn't account for the range of feelings which had swept through her as his arms had tightened around her. Yet to suppose she harboured any genuine emotions for the man whose mouth had momentarily wrought such certain magic upon her was absurd! She would never be a conquest for some entrepreneur with nothing on his mind but brief physical pleasure.

So she'd go to the races and play the part designated to her, because ill-advisedly she'd been talked into it and, as Alain had divined, she wouldn't break her word. Afterwards it was certain that the opinionated visitor from France would require nothing further from her— and that was exactly what she wanted. The strange hollow ache she felt inside her at the thought could only be due to the uncertainty of what faced her.

At one time the previous evening she'd toyed with the idea of getting her own back for his presumptuousness by dressing in jeans, a T-shirt and the old trainers she wore on her summertime walks across Wimbledon Common. For several minutes she'd imagined and delighted in his reaction to her appearing like a refugee from Joggers Anonymous. She'd had to abandon the idea, of course. Not only because she had a very real sense of occasion and took pleasure in dressing accordingly, but because she had a nasty suspicion that if she'd dared to flout his wishes he would have insisted she change—and more than likely have stood over her while she did so!

The mischievous thought of his invading her bedroom
and selecting a suitable outfit taunted her as she towelled
herself dry. Her pupils dilated, darkening as she relived
the feel of his hard, silky mouth against her own. It was
the first time she'd been kissed like that since her relationship with Andy had ended. Come to that, even
Andy had never kissed her with such a hint of controlled
passion—and certainly not after she'd only known him
for a few weeks!

Selecting an aerosol of expensive French body foam
from the bathroom cabinet, she pressed a glistening ball
of the substance into the palm of one hand and began
to smooth it into the sensitive skin of her warmly glowing
breasts. It was true, she admitted, what Andy had said
to her on their last evening together. If she'd really cared
for him she would have given up her job and gone back
to live in the town where he practised as a solicitor,
instead of limiting their meetings to the weekends.

She thought of him affectionately. Such a presentable
young man, public school, university educated, and very
easy to get on with. She'd known him for six months
when he'd proposed to her. Thoughtfully, she took more
foam, applying it the length of her body with firm, sure
strokes, breathing the perfume it released with sensual
pleasure. She had to admit she'd been tempted by the
proposal, aware she could have settled down quite
happily to the role of country solicitor's wife, raising a
family surrounded by a warm circle of family and
friends, if only...if only she had sensed that certain vital
spark between them that she'd always supposed existed
between a man and woman in love.

Andy had been dismayed and hurt by her gentle
refusal, accusing her of being a hard-headed career girl
obsessed with personal achievement and the bright lights

of London. His criticism had hurt, but she'd borne it
stoically, knowing it sprung from his wounded ego.

She did enjoy her job—and she was certainly committed to self-fulfilment, but the two things weren't
necessarily related. As for the bright lights! Like most
Londoners she found the high price of entertainment
heavy on her purse and not automatically to her liking.
The joy she found in the capital belonged more readily
to the beautiful, quiet Inns of Court behind the City,
the stretches of parkland and the ethereal beauty of the
Wren churches.

Only her legs now for the treatment. Running both
foam-covered palms over the shapely curves of her calves
and thighs, she smiled, recalling how Andy had apolo-
gised for his accusations and begged her to continue their
friendship on whatever basis she preferred. She'd done
so willingly, enjoying his company, indulging in light
lovemaking, hoping against hope that one day Andy
might discover and kindle the source of the hidden flame
she felt so sure existed deep within her just waiting for
the right man to uncover and coax into a blazing fire!

Just when she had been beginning to believe that she
was being unrealistically romantic Andy had proved her
right, by falling hopelessly and irrevocably in love with
Sandra. Divorced, with two young children and coming
from a background as different from his own as it was
possible to get, Sandra had shocked both his parents and
his business associates—and Andy hadn't given a damn!
That was love—and Alex envied them both!

Replacing the aerosol in the cabinet, satisfied that
every satin inch of her skin exuded a subtle scent, Alex
walked through into her bedroom and began to dress in
the clothes she'd chosen for the occasion. Over a black
body stocking and hi-line flesh-coloured nylon tights she
pulled on a black cashmere sweater with a high neck. It

had been a bargain buy in one of the Knightsbridge sales
and she'd never regretted investing in it. Soft and
beautiful, it had kept its shape and texture through many
hand-washings and was the ideal top to wear beneath
the Chanel-style black and white nubbly wool tweed suit
she'd made herself.

Of course, it wasn't a fashionable meeting, but she
knew the classic suit with its up-to-date blocked shoulder-
line and figure-skimming lines would not be out of place.
Accessories had proved no problem—black leather shoes
with a Cuban heel which wouldn't pin her into the turf,
matching gloves and a satchel-type handbag also in the
ubiquitous black leather would finish the ensemble to
her satisfaction—and hopefully Alain's as well!

Placing a towel round her shoulders, she regarded her
un-made-up face critically in the mirror. No one could
accuse her of being a raving beauty—but at least she had
an unblemished and unremarkable canvas on which to
work! Deftly she applied a pale foundation to her blonde
skin, dusting it with a light powder. No need for blusher,
she decided ruefully. The cheeks of her long, oval face
were already glowing from the warmth of her bath, quite
apart from the fact that she'd rediscovered her natural
tendency to blush, her emotions betrayed far more easily
than she would have preferred by the natural translu-
cency of her skin. Not for the first time did she wish
she had a thick, creamy skin which would mask the
passage of her feelings.

Sighing, she stared back into her own eyes. Probably
her best feature, she decided without vanity. They were
large, well-shaped and widely spaced, the blue irises
ringed with a still darker blue. All they needed was a
touch of pale grey and charcoal eyeshadow on the lids
to enhance and deepen them. A light brown mascara
thickened and darkened the sweep of eyelashes sur-

rounding them, while a trace of pencil on her flaring eyebrows gave them more substance. All that was left to do was to apply a touch of pale pink lipstick to her mouth before giving her final attention to her hair.

As she unwound the protective towel from her head she sent a mental vote of thanks to Martine for her advice. It had been the other girl who'd recommended she had a body wave applied to her fine, fly-away mane, with the result that the silky mass had been tamed into submission, gently falling to frame her face, a wispy half-fringe softening the high forehead upon which it fell. A quick session with a hairbrush and she was ready for whatever the day might bring.

When the doorbell rang promptly at twelve-thirty she counted ten before walking sedately to the door and opening it.

'Ah! Ready to leave, I see!' Alain greeted her with satisfaction as she feasted her eyes on him. She'd been so occupied in arranging her own wardrobe, she hadn't given a thought to what he might be wearing. His casual trousers had been created by a master, fashionably tailored to the long length of his body with a loving regard for balance: above them the champagne-coloured open-necked sports shirt appeared to be made of silk, and the dark chestnut-coloured leather jacket which added breadth to his naturally wide shoulders was so soft and supple in appearance she fancied it must be made from antelope skin.

The effect was breathtaking. Truly it was said that clothes made the man, for with the forsaking of his formal business suit Alain du Gard seemed to have lost a great deal of the hauteur with which she normally associated him. He looked younger, far more approachable and astonishingly handsome.

'Do you approve?' he asked drily, leaving her in no doubt that he was aware of and amused by her frank regard.

'It's not my prerogative to judge,' she returned quickly. 'It's I who should be asking you that question.'

She'd asked for his assessment so she could hardly resent the minute inspection to which he subjected her. Totally comprehensive, his appraisal fell short of insolence as she tensed beneath his sweeping regard. Why then did she feel as if she were standing there naked, a tiny tremor shivering its way from her golden head to her shapely feet while she awaited his verdict?

'Well?' she prompted, her voice sharpening with tension at his prolonged silence. 'If you'd prefer me to wear something different...?'

'No, no, not at all.' The timbre of his voice was low and full, almost a purr. 'On the contrary—you're exactly what I had in mind. Shall we go, Alex?'

She liked Dudley and Liz on sight. Dudley was a great bear of a man, tall and broad-shouldered, a thick shock of silver hair brushed back from his fresh-complexioned face belying his sixty years of age. Liz, at least fifteen years his junior, was a slender, graceful woman with short dark curling hair and an infectious smile. Not the kind of person to be hurt or bored if left to her own devices, Alex assessed perceptively, which made Alain's plans even more puzzling.

Fortunately he'd briefed her very thoroughly on the way down to the course, filling her in on the intricacies of racing as he'd manoeuvred his Jaguar XJS skilfully through the traffic.

'Although I must admit,' he'd told her with refreshing candour, 'I'm out of touch with English form, so don't look to me to provide you with winners!'

'No problem,' she'd replied flippantly. 'I'll just choose a name I like.'

'Probably as good a way as any.' Surprisingly he hadn't mocked her suggestion. 'Naturally you won't be expected to finance your own bets as you're on company business. Just let me know what you fancy and I'll do the rest.'

She'd nodded her thanks. Although she suspected she'd have been quite content wandering about just watching the horses and the crowds without venturing her hard-earned money on any speculative outcome, in retrospect she could see that course of action would have been too naïve for Alain and his friends.

As the afternoon progressed she found she was enjoying herself tremendously. Preliminary drinks were followed by a lunch consisting of soup, cold chicken salad, and cheese with biscuits accompanied by wine, while the race cards were studied and discussed. Thanks to Alain's instruction Alex found herself able to read both the card and the *Sporting Life* with an intelligent perception.

Four races later she'd had the satisfaction of picking one long-priced winner and two good-priced places. For a beginner that wasn't too bad, she congratulated herself.

'You must be proud of this lass of yours!' Dudley slapped Alain on the back with friendly enthusiasm. 'She's got a darn sight better eye for a good thing than I have.'

'Oh, I am,' came Alain's guileless reply as he dropped an arm to encircle her waist. 'Alex is a bright girl indeed when it comes to choosing winners. She should go far in life.'

'As far as Paris perhaps?' Liz teased him, being rewarded with a quick smile and a nonchalant 'Who knows?' before he sauntered away to join Dudley, who had reseated himself at their table, head bent over the *Sporting Life.*

'The paddock!' Alex exclaimed hurriedly, not keen for Liz to continue with her veiled queries. 'Do you think we could go and watch the runners parade for the next race?'

Liz wrinkled her pretty nose. 'To be honest with you, these shoes of mine are a bit tight and the walk could cripple me. Why don't you ask Alain to take you down?'

'Oh, I don't think . . .' On the point of voicing her disinclination to disturb him, Alex paused, a spark of devilment flickering inside her. Although Dudley and Alain had spent a brief time with their heads together discussing business, it hadn't been enough to discomfit Liz, Alex was sure, which meant her presence there hadn't been necessary at all. Her original intention of having a little fun at Alain's expense resurfaced. After all, he'd asked her to treat him as a personal friend; perhaps the time had come to add a little spice to the act.

He'd taken advantage of the warmth of the day to remove his jacket, and Alex was very conscious of the breadth of his shoulders under the fine silk of the beautifully tailored shirt as she approached him.

With a deliberate sense of fun she placed the palm of her hand lightly beneath the collar-line of his shirt, then allowed it to creep in a steady undulating movement to his shoulder-joint, where she pressed her fingers into the hard bone.

'Alain,' she breathed, her face deliciously close to his as she inhaled the sharp scent of aftershave. 'Alain, *chéri,* could you take me to the paddock, please?'

She'd felt his skin quiver at her first touch, but nothing in his tone confirmed it. 'Mmm. Just a moment, *chérie.*' His brow furrowed in concentration, he continued reading the paper. Determined not to be ignored, Alex sighed dramatically, allowing her hand to drift down his arm until the palm rested on his left forearm as it lay relaxed on the table.

In an instant it was covered by Alain's own right hand, his fingers moving with a deadly purpose up the cuff of her jacket.

'Alain?' Her voice voice shook a little, because, although he still seemed only half aware of her presence, the fingers warm and predatory inside her jacket were telling a different story, finding their way beneath the soft cuff of her sweater to explore the tender skin of her inner arm above the wrist.

Sensuous, insidious, their presence was incredibly disturbing. Never in her life had she been so aware of the structure of her own arms as Alain's caressing fingers touched and awakened each sensitive cell beneath the skin.

Who would have thought he'd turn the tables on her like this? She shot a wary glance at his face but it remained impassive.

'Alain?' Her mouth dry, she repeated his name a little desperately. 'Please!' She was pleading for the hidden torment to cease, but he chose to interpret her plea in his own way.

'Sorry, Dudley. You'll have to work this one out by yourself. Alex is keen to visit the paddock.'

Much to her surprise she was actually trembling as he removed his hand from her wrist and rose to his feet with a look of absolute innocence on his face to lead her towards the lifts.

Once out of sight of the Moorheads, Alex shrugged off his embrace. 'No one's watching now,' she told him tautly, wondering what could have possessed her to bait him.

'Careful, Alex,' he warned softly. 'The strain of pretending to like me is beginning to show.'

'Probably,' she agreed crisply, glad of an opportunity to assert herself. 'I don't care for being used for business purposes.'

The incident at the table had upset her more than she liked to admit to herself, and she was angry with herself for having provoked it. Dear heavens! The movement of his fingers on her skin had made her feel as if she had no control over her own reactions. How else to explain the increased rhythm of her heart and the sudden warmth engendered in her veins? What was even worse— she had a sneaking feeling that Alain was not unaware of the result of his action!

'Then I shall have to find some other purpose for which to use you,' he told her equably.

She shot him a reproachful look. 'You know exactly what I mean.'

'Of course I do.' He chose deliberately to misunderstand her. 'You aren't enjoying yourself.'

With an effort she swallowed her indignation at his overt attempt to misinterpret her meaning, deciding not to argue with him.

'It's hardly my scene,' she agreed tersely. Then, glancing at the strong line of his profile, she added indifferently, 'I suppose you go racing a lot in France?'

'Sometimes to Longchamps or Auteuil,' he said, nodding. 'I have an apartment in Passy near the Bois de Boulogne, which means both Paris courses are on my doorstep.' He considered the classic line of her cheek and chin, his gaze lingering on the mascaraed sweep of long lashes that masked the expression in her eyes. 'But I'm no gambler. Although that's not to say I don't enjoy trying to select winners.'

Irritated by his courteous poise, and still unsettled by the liberties his fingers had taken, Alex tried to needle him. 'As you select women?' she taunted. 'By studying their past performance, appraising their fitness and seeing if they're suitable for the outing you have in mind?'

She was rewarded by a long, thoughtful stare from narrowed yes. 'That, *ma chère* Alex, would rather depend on what I was selecting them for. Now, if it was for a job, I think that would describe my attitude quite neatly—although of course...' the corner of his mouth lifted mockingly '... I've been known to make mistakes. It's not unusual for a beautiful-looking filly to fail in a trial situation.'

Sensitive to his tone, Alex sucked in her breath as his cool, supercilious gaze swept over her, stripping her of self-confidence. 'Are you saying you're disappointed with my performance today?' she demanded, angered by his comprehensive stock-taking of her assets and exasperated by the suggestion she had failed him in some way.

Tawny eyes flickered at her obvious resentment with what she judged to be a hint of pleasure.

'Good heavens, Alex!' He raised suitably astonished eyebrows. 'I thought we were just generalising!'

Did you indeed? she thought, aware that she'd just betrayed her vulnerability to his opinion, and also that he was speaking with little regard for the truth. They'd been playing a game of words and he'd emerged a worthy winner.

She felt his fingers tighten round her upper arm as he guided her towards the distant paddock, resolutely refusing to register the way her body stiffened in protest at his intimate touch.

'Now,' he continued, smoothly, 'if you want to know how I select a woman for a personal relationship, well, that's a little different.' He paused as if challenging her to speak. Well, he would wait all day. What possible interest could the matter be to her?

'In such a case,' he continued, apparently in no way discouraged by her silence, 'I like them to be physically beautiful, classically bred and never saddled by another owner.'

He looked at her expectantly, challenging her comment.

'Fancy!' Alex swallowed her indignation at this glaring chauvinism, aware she was being goaded for his pleasure, and determined not to rise to his bait. 'I wonder how often you're successful in finding what you want.'

'Not nearly often enough, *ma chérie*,' came the dry retort. '*Viens, alors*! Let's find this paddock before the next race starts.'

CHAPTER FIVE

'THAT was delicious.' Several hours after the last race
had finished, Alex sat across a small table from Alain
in the restaurant of a rambling, Tudor-styled public
house, set deep in the Surrey countryside, Dudley and
Liz having left earlier for the long drive back to
Yorkshire.

'Would you like another one?' Alain regarded her
enquiringly.

'Heavens, no—it's quite intoxicating.' She drifted the
tip of her tongue round her lips tasting the sharp, spirited
sweetness of the Grand Marnier liqueur in which her
dessert of fresh orange slices had been marinated.

Conscious of Alain's gaze on her mouth, and finding
his intense interest disquieting, she forced herself to speak
casually. 'What a pity Liz and Dudley couldn't spare the
time to join us.'

'Yes, indeed.' His voice was serious enough, but his
golden eyes mocked her. He was clearly not in the least
concerned about their absence. Neither had he made any
effort to put their own relationship back on a businesslike footing. In fact, over an excellent meal accompanied by a bottle of dry white wine she'd almost
forgotten she was only there on sufferance.

Sipping the full, mellow wine, she felt herself relax.
To be honest she was finding it very pleasant to be
escorted by this good-looking Frenchman, who for the
past couple of hours had acted the perfect host and
companion.

Aware of a feeling of elation, she looked away from him, telling herself to be careful—not to trust this pulsing excitement which was making her limbs tremble. It was probably a reflex reaction to the thrill of the races, the excitement of a close finish, the beauty of such strong, graceful animals moving so freely... It had nothing to do with Alain personally. He was but a passing influence in her life—arguably charming, physically and mentally stimulating, but above all impermanent!

'Alex...' His voice was strangely taut as his hand moved to cover her own on the table. Startled, she realised she'd been stroking the neck of the wine bottle, running her thumb round its open top, caressing its long, slender neck with convulsive movements of her slim fingers.

Embarrassed, she withdrew her hand. Good grief! She'd been behaving like a bored child playing with the things on the table. Whatever would he make of her nervous behaviour? But there was nothing critical in his expression as he leaned towards her, his voice oddly husky.

'Do you want a liqueur with your coffee?'

'Oh, no—thank you.' She wasn't used to drinking. True, the amount of wine she'd had with her lunch was hardly excessive, and she'd barely noticed what she'd just finished with dinner. Nevertheless, she was beginning to feel decidedly off-key. Enough was enough, she told herself firmly. The sudden warmth of emotion she was experiencing for Alain du Gard must be due to some external cause—and she could only blame the alcohol.

Hurriedly she rose to her feet. 'I think I'll find the cloakroom and freshen up a bit!'

Taking her time, she repaired her make-up, brushing her hair and trying to regain her composure. Adrenalin seemed to be flowing through her system at an increased rate, making her heart pound and her mouth dry. The 'fight or flight' hormone, she accorded wryly, wondering if her body was trying to tell her something.

When at last she did return it was to find Alain walking away from the reception desk. He approached her with his relaxed, easy stride, saying coolly, 'I've just been enquiring about getting rooms here tonight.'

Totally taken aback, Alex stared at him speechlessly.

'Look,' he said simply, 'I've had some very late nights recently and I honestly feel too tired to drive back to London tonight. Besides,' he gave a small self-deprecating grimace, 'I've probably had more than the legal limit to drink.'

Filled with sudden apprehension, she regarded him with suspicious eyes. 'You're not drunk! Why, you haven't had much more than I have!'

'Look, Alex . . .' He didn't intend to argue, she could tell from the arrogant note that had crept back into his voice. 'I'm sorry, but there it is. If you like I'll send you home by hired car. On the other hand they can offer us a couple of suites here for the night. It seems they're used to putting up people attending courses at the executive training centre in the nearby town, and are able to offer us very civilised accommodation. So how about it?'

Alex swallowed hastily, looking away, unable to meet the gentle irony of his expression. To refuse point-blank would make her seem very unsophisticated, and he had said a couple of suites . . .

'But I've no luggage,' she said at last.

'However much do you need for one night?' The derision in the question infuriated her.

'Well, certainly a toothbrush!' she snapped. And that was all really. She could easily sleep naked and rinse out her nylon bodyshaper in the handbasin, drying it by whatever form of heating was supplied.

'Then you're in luck. I've got a spare.'

'I don't believe you!' She turned incredulous eyes on his smug expression.

'I swear it.' He lifted a hand as if taking an oath. 'I've still got the weekend case I took to Bradford with me. There's a toilet kit in it with two of everything. You're welcome to the spare toothbrush.' He regarded her, his dark head a little to one side, his expression unreadable.

Every instinct warned her to refuse his offer, yet the cool words of rejection refused to pass her lips. Instead she heard herself say with an air of detachment, 'I'd have to make a phone call. I've already made arrangements for this evening.'

She'd promised to call in on Tony and Martine to recount the day's adventures. If she failed to put in an appearance they would worry about her.

'Nothing too binding, I trust?' Alain was watching her closely, a slight smile softening the strong line of his jaw.

She gave a resigned shrug of her shoulders. 'Nothing that can't be postponed.'

Several hours later as she entered her suite, her watch confirmed it was half-past eleven. The accommodation was delightful: a enormous double-bedded room, amply furnished with its own bathroom leading off. Her mouth curved into a smile as she turned over one of the tooth glasses on the glass ledge and placed Alain's spare brush in it. Her sole piece of luggage!

Placing the plug in the bath, she turned on the mixer tap before returning to the bedroom, methodically removing her suit and hanging it in the large wardrobe provided.

How pleasantly the evening had passed. She allowed her thoughts to stray back to it as she began to strip off her remaining clothes. After her phone call she and Alain had taken their coffee into the residents' lounge, a spacious room with intimately placed groups of armchairs.

She'd been pleasantly flattered by what appeared to be his genuine interest in her parents and their recent decision to take a couple of years' holiday in Canada with their son. Relaxing beneath his gentle questioning, she'd told him about Jamie's family, even producing from her handbag the photographs of her nieces.

'You never thought of going over there yourself?' he'd asked with raised eyebrows.

'It would be a bit of a strain on my budget and it doesn't seem fair to ask for leave of absence from the bank which would make the journey worthwhile,' she'd said honestly. 'Although I do miss Jamie quite a lot. He's six years older than I am—and we've always been good friends despite the gulf of age and sex between us!'

She knew the affection she felt for her brother must have shown in her face as she'd detailed how Jamie had followed the family tradition of medicine, meeting his wife-to-be, Sara, at medical school where she'd been studying clinical psychology. As soon as he'd qualified Jamie had seen his career in Canada and Sara had abandoned her own career to marry him, go with him and bear his children. Yes, she had admitted, she missed her brother, but she was overjoyed for the happiness he had discovered.

It was then Alain had told her about his own sister, Giselle, just two years younger than himself, and her husband Gerard. He'd spoken with obvious fondness, describing the lovely home they owned on the outskirts of Paris and the enchanting niece and nephew he had.

'Soon to be added to, I might add,' he'd told her. 'I expect to be made an uncle for the third time quite soon now.'

The idea had seemed to please him, Alex pondered, although for the life of her she couldn't imagine him at ease in the company of children. How would he cope with sticky fingers on his beautiful suits, or spilt black-currant juice on his spotless shirts? Probably, she conceded after a moment's thought, Giselle's children were always immaculate and such problems didn't arise.

Oddly enough she'd had to fight a sudden temptation to tell him about Martine and Tony and all the heart-break they'd suffered. Fortunately she'd resisted it. Alain had just been showing a polite interest in her, but he would hardly be enthralled by the life story of her friends, would he? Besides, Tony's and Martine's grief was their own—not to be shared with a stranger.

Dear heavens! She was tired. She tested the temperature of the bath before removing her last item of clothing and consigning it to the handbasin filled with warm soapy water. Stepping into the bath, she slid down into the warm water, sighing luxuriously.

She'd been there about ten minutes, just soaking and reliving the highlights of the day, when she heard the knock on the bedroom door. Damn! Clambering out, she looked around for something to cover her nakedness, thankfully settling on one of the large bath towels. Who on earth could want her at this hour? Heaven forbid anything had happened to Martine! Winding the towel tightly round her body, she padded on bare feet to the door.

'Yes?' she demanded tentatively.

'*C'est moi*, Alex.' The deep-toned voice was unmistakable even without the use of its native language. 'I've brought something for you.'

'Oh, Alain...' She was both relieved yet startled, unwilling to reveal herself to him with her hair damply curling round a face devoid of make-up. 'Can't it wait until morning?'

'Definitely not.' His voice was cool and autocratic. A voice that had impressed a board of dissenting directors in its time! 'Hurry up—there's a good girl!' He sounded businesslike and matter-of-fact.

'Oh, very well.' She slipped the catch off the door, turning the handle and retreating behind it, anchoring the towel more firmly.

He strode into the room, glancing round, surprised to find it seemingly empty. It was only when Alex pushed the door shut behind him and he spun round that he saw her standing there. To do him justice, he did look taken aback by her appearance.

'Did I get you out of the bath, Alex? I'm terribly sorry.' Only somehow the glowing amber eyes didn't look sorry at all—amused, interested, calculating, but not sorry. 'I brought this for you.'

Beneath her embarrassed gaze he unzipped the large silk envelope he was holding, taking out a folded piece of material, shaking it out to reveal a man's silk dressing-gown.

'A present from Giselle,' he told her. 'It's never been worn and it just occurred to me you could use it as a nightdress. It'll be warmer than cold cotton sheets, particularly for one person sleeping alone in a double bed.'

'How kind of you. Thank you.' Anxious to see him leave, she took the gown from him, moving towards the door, preparing to dismiss him graciously.

'Why don't you put it on now?' He nodded towards the bathroom. 'I'm sure you'll feel more comfortable, and there's something else I have to talk to you about.'

He moved away from her, seating himself in one of the armchairs provided, leaning back and closing his eyes.

What now? She bit her lip in frustration. Surely there couldn't be anything else that couldn't wait till the morning? On the other hand she would feel much less vulnerable wearing a proper garment instead of a towel. With a little sigh of despair she walked towards the bathroom, peering over her shoulder when she reached the door. Alain sat where he'd subsided, the picture of an exhausted man; not a muscle moved; his eyes were still closed.

She emerged a few seconds later enveloped from neck to below knee in expensive Yves St Laurent-designed silk, tantalisingly aware of the unbelievably erotic sensation of the slippery fabric against her nakedness.

'Something else, you said?' she queried politely, too aware of his dangerous male aura even in his present state of repose for her own peace of mind.

'Yes, yes, indeed.' He held out a hand as if he were asking her to help him to his feet. Unthinkingly she took it and tugged gently. 'I forgot to thank you for your help today—and to kiss you goodnight.'

Before she'd realised his intention he'd reversed the flow of energy between them, pulling her down easily on to his lap, reaching up with his other hand and guiding her head down so their lips met.

Hungrily, self-indulgently, his mouth parted her shocked lips, attacking with an urgent persistence against her instinctive defence. Even as she struggled she felt a warm spiral of need rising within her still-damp body, making it impossible for her to deny him the bold exploration of her mouth that he was seeking.

'Come on, my darling,' he muttered rawly, as, leaving her mouth tingling, he moved questing lips to trace a velvet path to the hollow of her throat. *'Grand Dieu!* How delicious you smell. Don't hold back from me, *bien-aimée*. I have wanted to do this all day! Heaven knows how much I want you!'

'Alain . . . please!' Bewildered by his ardency, trapped by his arms and horrified by the way her body appeared to be melting beneath his embrace, at that moment Alex lacked the physical strength to repulse him.

If he even heard her protest he ignored it, causing her to tense in alarm as he emitted a long, shuddering sigh, moving slightly so she was lying half in the large chair and half across his taut, demanding body.

Somehow she had to stop this heady assault on her clamouring senses. His actions bore the outward signs of love but carried neither liking nor affection—just a raw, primitive need. Even though she experienced and understood its powerful stimulus, she knew there was no way she could allow herself to surrender to it and keep her self-respect. Alain might be paying for her day, but the night wasn't part of the deal, and he insulted her if he thought otherwise!

Increasing her resistance, she flattened her hand against his chest, but to no effect. Was it possible her protest hadn't even registered on his strong, demanding male body? That driven by desire he'd become impervious to the pressure she was exerting against him?

'No!' She moaned as his hand slipped inside the top of the dressing-gown, moving in slow provocation over the swelling, naked curve.

'Yes, yes, Alex!' he corrected her, whispering the contradiction against her mouth, stifling any further protest as his wicked hands continued their caresses.

She had to stop this, and now! Her life wasn't—had never been—geared towards casual sex, and this was for real! Alain was no boy to be satisfied with anything less than her total surrender. Even now he wouldn't take too kindly to being dismissed.

'No!' She shouted the word furiously, struggling hard against him, pulling her body back so sharply that she became the agent of her own pain as her breast was forcibly torn from the caress of his lips, which had left her mouth to discover an even sweeter haven.

'Alex, what is it?' He seemed genuinely bewildered and not a little angry as her voice penetrated his consciousness. 'What have I done?'

'Nothing that can't be mended,' she gasped. 'I'm sorry, but you have to leave.'

'Leave? But...' He shook his dark head, his eyes narrowing speculatively. Then he laughed, a soft, knowing laugh that made the small hairs on the back of her neck rise. 'A token battle? Is that what this is all about?'

'Of course not.' She denied it with a voice that shook. 'I want——'

'Let me stay the night with you, Alex.' It was a whispered plea, as he released her from his hold, not even waiting for her to finish her sentence.

Taking the opportunity to scramble to her feet, drawing the disturbed robe tightly round her trembling body she fought to keep her voice steady. 'I—I'm sorry, Alain. No, you can't stay.' She swallowed hard, watching in alarm as the warmth of his golden eyes dissipated, to be replaced by a stoniness that appalled her. Desperately she struggled on, 'I'm sorry if anything I did or said made you think I wanted this...'

For twenty seconds he stared at her face, his expression enigmatic, then he uncurled his long length from the chair, stood up and stretched. The movement, so graceful yet menacing like an animal preparing for action, had her moving away from him, backing up against the wardrobe.

Two strides and he was in front of her, his arms passing over her shoulders, touching the wood against which she stood, imprisoning her, his face so close she could see the little lines of strain at the corners of his mouth, a tiny-triangle-shaped scar above his left eyebrow.

'All right, Alex.' There was a quiet purpose in his voice. 'But I'm not a brash teenager to be teased and abandoned without a protest, however beautiful the temptress may be.'

Shutting her eyes, she tried to keep out the remorseless condemnation that assailed her, wishing she could close her ears against his quiet, accusing voice as well. 'All evening you've been giving me signals. Invitations to make love to you—the way you ate—the way you drank...'

'What?' Her eyes shot open in astonishment, as a wave of warm sickness passed through her. 'You couldn't be more wrong!' she whispered, horror bleaching the colour from her face.

'I don't think so.' Alain regarded her speculatively. 'And when I kissed you, touched you... You wanted me just as much as I want you. Every part of your skin quickened to my hand and my mouth.' Mercilessly he justified himself.

Oh, how could he say such things to her? How dared he analyse, dissect the mysterious reactions of her body as if she were some balance sheet of a company he wanted to take over?

'Admit it, Alex,' he continued, his voice husky now, devoid of anger, as he stood so close to her his aura reached into her body space, flooding her with a painful awareness of his presence, the warm, clean male scent of him a powerful aphrodisiac even now when every part of her being wanted to repulse him. 'You have nothing to fear from me. I have never persuaded a reluctant virgin to act against her instincts. Naturally I respect your absolute right to change your mind, but don't lie to me!'

'I'm not——' she began heatedly.

'Of course not.' He truncated her sentence. 'The illustration was merely figurative, but the truth of it remains.'

Damn the man! He obviously thought she was contesting the label of 'virgin' instead of about to deny the accusation that she'd been lying.

'I was going to say,' she told him coldly, 'that, however excellent you consider yourself at judging a woman's response to you, no one is infallible, and on this occasion you've totally misread whatever signs you thought you'd seen. Now, I'd be obliged if you'd leave. I'm very tired and my only desire at this moment is to go to bed—alone... Monsieur du Gard.'

'Monsieur du Gard...' He repeated his own name musingly as he removed his entrapping arms, a strange glint sparkling in his amber eyes. 'So the masquerade is over, is it, Miss Hammond? Very well, if you so choose.'

She heaved a sigh of absolute relief as he made her a taut, formal little bow and began to move towards the door, only to feel her unstable pulse climb to a higher rate as he paused at the threshold.

'Before I go...' His hand moved to his hip pocket. Wide-eyed, Alex watched as he withdrew a roll of banknotes, peeling off five twenty-pound notes.

A hundred pounds—for what? Surely he wasn't putting a price on her company for the evening? White-faced, she stared at the money, refusing to take the proffered notes.

'Don't look so affronted, Miss Hammond.' His knowing eyes had guessed her thoughts, and it was obvious from his expression and the way he addressed her that her embarrassment pleased him. 'It's only what you won at the races.'

'And suppose I'd lost?' she demanded stiffly.

Topaz eyes passed over her silk-encased body, missing nothing. 'As I told you earlier, the bank would have borne your losses.'

'The bank—or you?' The thought of taking money from him was anathema to her.

Broad shoulders shrugged as he turned Louis XIV's famous phrase to his own use. '*La banque—c'est moi!*'

So he and the bank were the same thing, were they? She would have liked to dismiss his assertion as springing from illusions of grandeur, only somehow she thought his confidence was based on pretty firm ground.

'Take it, Alex,' he said softly. 'You won it fairly and squarely.'

'In that case, thank you.' She knew when she was beaten, and to accept with dignity was preferable to rejecting and giving the gesture far more import than it deserved.

'*Bon! Dors bien, ma chère.*' He let himself out of the room, closing the door gently behind him.

Sleep well! The wish was hardly likely to be fulfilled. The way she felt at the moment she'd be lucky to snatch more than a few disconnected hours!

When the alarm call Alain had arranged awakened her at seven o'clock the next morning, for a few moments she just lay there, staring at the ceiling, remembering the events of the previous day. Oddly enough, after about a quarter of an hour in which she'd tried to sort out her tumultuous emotions, she'd fallen asleep and enjoyed a dreamless repose.

Swinging her shapely legs out of the bed, she remained sitting on its edge. How much she'd enjoyed her time at the races, and afterwards at dinner she'd felt a growing intimacy between herself and the clever Frenchman who had demanded her company. Later, she admitted to herself, when they'd exchanged personal details over their coffee, she'd even felt a warm glow of liking for him, a growing rapport that only a few hours earlier she would have thought impossible.

Thoughtfully she rose to her feet and made for the bathroom. Fortunately she'd remembered to rinse out her underwear after Alain's departure and hung the delicate garment to dry by the hot-air vents that warmed the room. She touched the pretty nylon and lace with gentle fingers. If only she'd waited a little longer before having her bath, perhaps she wouldn't have given such a bold albeit unwitting invitation to Alain. Though from what he'd said he'd already assumed her easy compliance before even coming to her room.

Going through the motions of washing and dressing, she allowed her mind to dwell on the previous day's events. Had she encouraged him? Certainly not consciously, but in his company she had felt exhilarated. Everything had seemed a little brighter, the sky, the colour of the grass and trees, the shining coats of the racehorses. She'd been seeing the world through rose-coloured glasses, she supposed, and the question was—why?

Brushing her hair with the little handbag brush from her make-up kit, she stared at her pale reflection. Never one to turn her back on unpleasant facts, she found herself forced to admit how easy it would have been to love and be loved by Alain du Gard. For the first time in her life she'd found herself having to fight her own body's clamorous needs and the experience had shocked her.

Of course, she'd known all the time it would be impossible for her. Alain had made no secret of the fact that he assumed her to be experienced. She smiled wryly at her reflection. While she had every confidence in her natural responses, she would be the first to admit she was no advanced student in the art of love. If Alain had expected a graduate he would have been sorely disappointed—besides, she might be a moral dinosaur, but she would have felt dreadful this morning knowing she'd been treated like a *fille de joie*.

Not that she felt particularly happy anyway having to face *Monsieur le Directeur* over the breakfast table! What would his mood be? she wondered, competently applying a light make-up to her face. Hopefully he was a too well-adjusted personality to let a little thing like frustration sour him.

All right, so she'd been stupid, unworldly and far too trusting. As far as she knew none of those failings merited the death penalty! Satisfied that she looked as good as she could in the circumstances, she snapped her handbag shut with determination and went downstairs to the dining-room.

Alain was already there when she entered, rising attentively to his feet the moment she crossed the threshold. Fingers of sunlight arrowed through the mullioned windows, casting bars of light over the tables already prepared for breakfast. Dark oak walls and timbered beams added to the atmosphere of a leisurely bygone age, and the delicious smell from the kitchens assailed her nostrils. But it was none of these things which had her coming to a frozen halt while only a few paces inside the room.

Realisation struck her like a body-blow, stunning and barely believable. She loved Alain du Gard. *A clap of thunder*—wasn't that what the French called it? And the Spanish had a phrase about being struck by an arrow. She raised her eyes to Alain's politely enquiring face, gazing at him with a painful perception as the parts of the jigsaw fell into place.

For six weeks she'd worked with him, admiring his business skill, excited by his competence, yet always aware of a strange uncomfortable tension between them, an unspoken challenge she had longed to bring into the open, face and conquer. Love? Tony, sensitive to her moods, had suspected it. Love? Embryonic and unnourished because the object of it had remained aloof as if deliberately choosing to keep his distance from her— until his return from Bradford. That had been the beginning of a subtle change in his behaviour, but until the day before yesterday she had imagined him married, forbidden, her sense of moral rectitude acting as an iron censor on her emotions, refusing to let her evaluate them fairly.

Last night she'd been furious at his claim that she'd encouraged him—could it have been true? Her mind in utter turmoil, she could only look at him as if he were a stranger... Love!

'Are you all right, Alex?' She watched him walk towards her, concern marring the smooth lift of his forehead with a staff of lines.

'Yes, yes, I'm fine,' she lied, finding her voice and the power of movement simultaneously. 'I—I just thought of something I should have done at the office.'

'Well, I'm sure it can wait.' He cast her a curious look, escorting her back to the table. Thankfully she sank down on the seat, glad there were no other occupants in the restaurant, her quick eyes registering that he was wearing a clean shirt. His emergency travel kit was obviously well stocked—an obvious advantage to the amorously inclined businessman, she thought, fighting down a sudden twinge of jealousy.

'I didn't order because I wasn't sure whether you'd prefer coffee or tea,' he told her casually.

'Coffee suits me very well.' She smiled briefly at him before turning her attention to the waiter who had appeared beside her.

'And to eat, madam?' A menu was proffered.

Her initial reaction was to wave it away; on the other hand, the realisation of her own emotional state seemed to have stimulated her appetite. Either that or the savoury aromas emanating from the kitchen had titillated her salivary glands.

'Sausage, bacon, with toast and marmalade to follow, please. Oh, and orange juice to begin with.'

She settled herself comfortably in her chair, watching Alain's serious face as he ordered coffee and toast for himself.

'Alex, about last night . . .' he began hesitantly as soon as the waiter disappeared.

It was what she'd been dreading. A post-mortem. Now was the time to pretend a sophistication she was far from feeling.

'I think it's for the best if we both forget it, don't you?' she asked brightly.

'I certainly think we should start afresh,' he agreed to her relief. 'If only because last night I gave you the impression I wanted to be your lover.'

She didn't dispute the indisputable, glad that the waiter chose that moment to supply the orange juice and coffee. A wayward disappointment surged through her as she anticipated his words. He was going to say that in the cold light of day he'd changed his mind and wanted to assure her wouldn't sully whatever remained of their working relationship with personal approaches. What more could she expect? He had seen her as providing a night's amusement and she had no one but herself to blame after her stupid behaviour both on the racecourse and afterwards! She took a deep draught of orange juice in an attempt to compose her expression as the waiter departed.

'Alex...' He waited for her to replace the glass on the table before reaching across and taking her hand. 'The truth is I want more than that. Much more. I want you to marry me.'

CHAPTER SIX

SHOCK paralysed the muscles of Alex's throat, making it impossible for her either to swallow or speak. Alain had to be joking! But it wasn't amusing. It was probably the most cruel thing he could have said to her when she hadn't even begun to come to terms with the revelation of her own feelings, but then he didn't know how she was feeling, did he?

'That's not very funny,' she told him in a stifled voice, when she found herself able to use it once more, her fevered mind searching for and finding an explanation. 'Playing the part of your girlfriend didn't turn out very successfully did it? I'm sorry, but whatever pressure you try and bring on me, there's no way I'll agree to pretend to be your wife, however important the business deal.'

'Who's talking pretence or business deals, Alex?' His eyes mesmerised her, draining away her antagonism, as she continued to stare at him, the only stable focus in a room that was suddenly unreal. 'I'm quite serious. Think about it. I can give you gowns by St Laurent, you may have your choice of the Caribbean for a honeymoon— even a Lamborghini wouldn't bankrupt me.'

She shook her head, doubting what her ears were telling her as he continued forcefully, 'You'd have a good life as my wife, Alex. Apart from my apartment in Paris I own a holiday villa in Corscia and I'm in the process of buying a mansion in the Bois de Boulogne. You know Paris and, by your own admission, love it. As Madame du Gard you will have as busy a social life as you desire. Invitations will pour in on you from all sides! Then

87

there's Giselle. She will be overjoyed to have a sister-in-law, a confidante, and I feel sure you will like her.'

'Is she like you?' Alex asked faintly, unable to think of anything more constructive to say at that point.

'No.' Alain smiled. 'She's much prettier and much nicer—a generous woman and a loyal friend.'

'She sounds quite special.'

'She is—so what do you say?'

Thankfully she was spared an immediate answer as her breakfast was put in front of her. Obviously he meant what he said. If she had any sense she would refuse instantly to consider the idea, yet one part of her wanted to throw herself into his arms and declare that she loved him and wanted to spend the rest of her life with him. The other, more cautious side of her nature counselled discretion.

Was it true that absence made the heart grow fonder, and during his stay in Bradford he'd realised that despite the difference in their business 'rank' he had fallen in love with her? Could it be that his feelings had burst on him with the same cataclysmic effect that had actioned her own? Perhaps he'd even intended to take things along at a more sedate pace until what he had seen as her encouragement during the afternoon. Then last night when her body had betrayed her...

Yes, she thought, that was the way it had happened, taking him by surprise as much as it had her, but being who and what he was he'd acted immediately—seen what he'd wanted, made his offer, even sugaring the sweetness of himself with mention of the material benefits he could supply as if she would be influenced by cars or houses if she didn't already love him! But then, used to difficult negotiations, he would always have something in reserve to make his point...

'But we've only known each other a few weeks,' she said breathlessly, her thoughts spinning uncontrollably.

'What has time to do with it?' He looked genuinely surprised. 'A marriage is a contract between two people who wish to join their lives for mutual gain. When the desire is there—the time is right, *non*?'

'Like Triple I?' she asked helplessly, and was rewarded by his soft smile.

'An excellent example, *ma chère*. The merger they have undertaken will bring them nothing but future success and prosperity, and you and I had a hand in that.' A sudden huskiness deepened his voice. 'We work well together, Alex. We get results. Many a marriage has been built on flimsier ground, besides which, of course...' he leant across the table towards her so that she was transfixed by his nearness, the powerful aura of the predatory male '...we are not incompatible on a physical level either, are we?'

The rise of blood to her cheeks supplied the answer her lips refused to make, as he leaned back again in his chair. 'I learned this morning that I have to return to Paris at the earliest possible opportunity, and I should like to take you back with me as my wife, which is one of the reasons I've sprung the idea on you so suddenly.' He smiled wryly. 'The fact that you haven't already turned me down flat makes me feel optimistic, I must confess.'

'You're leaving London!' She thought of life at the bank without him, and found the prospect intolerable but still caution acted as a brake. 'It's just that I find your proposal so...so unbelievable!' She was not normally unable to deal with unexpected occurrences, and her inability to get her mind working logically in this instance had left her at a distinct disadvantage. Alain, drinking his coffee, was much more composed, but then he was undoubtedly much more sophisticated than she was.

'Why? Take a look in a mirror, *ma chère*. You are beautiful and elegant. Your voice is sweet and your intellect sharp, you appreciate good food and fine wines—we speak the same language in more ways than one...'

It was a catalogue of virtues taken from a dating magazine and instinctively she resented its suavity. 'And I'm classically bred and have never been saddled by another owner?' she retorted fiercely.

'Precisely!' His mouth turned in a wicked, heart-breaking smile, but his eyes remained intense, their focus on her own. 'And when I left you last night I knew I had to possess you by fair means or foul—and since my reputation precludes the foul...'

'What about the rest of your family?' she asked hesitantly, amazed at herself because she was actually considering this wild proposal. 'Are your parents still alive? What will they think if you take back an English bride they've never even heard of, let alone met?'

'My mother will never know. My father divorced her when I was five years old, and I've never set eyes on her since.' His expression darkened, the muscles of his face tensing against unhappy memories. 'As for my father...' He shrugged his shoulders in typical Gallic fashion. 'I haven't seen him for fifteen years, ever since I chose finance as an alternative career to viticulture when I was nineteen. His opinion matters nothing to me.'

He must have seen her lips part in protest, for he added harshly, 'Your breakfast's getting cold, Alex, and we should be making a start for London soon. You don't have to give me your answer directly. I realise you have—commitments—which will need to be dealt with, but none, I hope, so binding that it will prevent you from giving my proposal your serious consideration.'

Silently Alex returned her attention to her breakfast, only able to toy with the food. In fact she had very few commitments. With Lindy having recently started a relationship with a Texan rancher, it was likely she wouldn't be returning to England, so the flat they shared could be easily disposed of. As for her parents—well, Paris wasn't the other side of the globe. She was dearly fond of them, but she'd be likely to see them just as frequently in France as she would if she stayed in England. By the same token, she wouldn't have to lose the many friends she still had in Hampshire.

Finishing breakfast in silence, she wondered if it was the caffeine in the coffee that had set her heart beating at breakneck speed or the charge of adrenalin that Alain's proposal had sent flowing through her veins. He hadn't actually said he loved her, but his behaviour yesterday when coupled with an offer of marriage could leave no doubt in her mind that he did! With a growing sense of excitement she realised she was more than halfway to making her decision, as her eyes sought the face of the dynamic, clever man who sat opposite her seemingly lost in a world of his own as he drank his coffee.

One hundred and eighty pounds of bone and muscle and sinew, she guessed, fashioned into the form of a man, and what a man! Tall, well-formed with the face of a crusader, determined, proud and handsome. Last night she'd blossomed beneath his touch, sensed his passion and resolve. Already she knew of his business acumen, his punctilious manners, his reputation in an exacting and respected career.

What she didn't know was his soul, what made him laugh or cry, what excited him or drove him to despair. She knew he was tough—he had to be to have survived in Paris alone at nineteen and to have studied so diligently with all the attractions of the capital beckoning him. He was also unforgiving, or perhaps capable of the unforgivable, to have remained alienated from his father all those years.

The truth was she loved what she did know and possessed a stirring desire to discover his latent depths, to nurture and comfort him when he was in pain and to be by his side and share his triumphs. Something clear and cold inside her, untouched by either reason or emotion, told her Alain was her destiny, and, if that wasn't a good enough basis for agreeing to marry him, what was?

It wasn't unheard of either for a couple to meet, fall in love and wed within a few weeks, was it? Not typical of the cool, poised Alex Hammond to make such an important decision on the spur of the moment—but then, that was what love was all about! If she couldn't give him his answer now, another week would make no difference.

'Are you ready to leave?' He broke into her reverie, catching and holding her wide-eyed glance.

'Yes, surely. Alain...'

'Mmm?' He paused in the act of rising from the table.

'If—if you're really sure it's what you want, then, yes. Yes, I'll marry you.'

For several seconds their gazes remained locked, hers tentative but unwavering, his flatteringly exultant.

'Oh, yes, Alex,' he said softly at last. 'I'm quite sure.'

Under the pressure of Martine's thumbs the cork from the champagne bottle hit the ceiling.

'*Vite, vite*, Alex!' she commanded as the bubbling wine effervesced from the dark-necked bottle.

'Oh, Martine!' Obediently Alex placed her glass under the bottle. 'A vintage year too...'

'And why not?' Martine's eyes were damp with emotion. 'As soon as you phoned me this morning I put it in the fridge. For a special occasion only, yes?' She smiled brightly. 'And what better than the news that you and Alain du Gard are to be married in ten days' time?'

Swallowing the cold, foaming liquid, enjoying its delicious bouquet and its tart flavour, Alex knew it had been purchased with the idea of celebrating a birth rather than a marriage, but she had more tact than to remark on it.

'I'm intoxicated enough without this,' she volunteered. 'Honestly, you can't imagine what the last twelve hours have been like. What with phoning Mum and Dad in Canada, Lindy in the States and my friends in Hampshire——'

'It's a good job you don't come from a large family.' Martine looked at her affectionately. 'You would have been on the phone all day.'

'Yes, I know.' Alex took a deep draught of the champagne. 'As it is we've decided on a quiet wedding—especially as neither my parents nor Jamie will be able to come. I was hoping they'd be able to fly back for the ceremony. Alain wanted to pay their fares, but, as Dad told me, there was already a letter in the post telling me about Mum's accident—how she'd broken her leg, which of course makes it impossible for her to travel.'

Luckily her mother was more inconvenienced by the result of her accident than anything else, assuring Alex that there was no need to worry. Predictably she'd been incredulous then tearful at hearing her daughter's news, while Dr Hammond had been cheerfully resigned. Jamie, contacted at a hotel in the States, had been unrestrainedly delighted at his sister's sudden decision, telling her cheerfully that he was beginning to think she'd never find a man good enough for her! Even he, successful and established in his own career, had expressed admiration at Alain's business pedigree!

'It's maddening about Jamie,' Martine sympathised. 'Fancy being away on a medical seminar in Miami, and for three weeks as well!'

'Sickening, isn't it?' Alex smiled ruefully. 'It's just as if fate is conspiring against us, but still, I must admit I did give them all very short notice. Besides, Alain has promised me that as soon as he can make the time we'll fly over to Canada for a grand reunion.'

'Well, that's something to look forward to.' Martine took a sanguine view, her dark eyes sparkling with happiness at her friend's obvious joy. 'I suppose Alain's family will be coming over?'

'Actually, no.' Alex's smile faltered. 'He's lost touch with his mother and apparently his father says he's not well enough to travel.' It had been at her insistence that the invitation had been passed to François du Gard, only to be regretted when the curt refusal had been passed to her via his housekeeper. Alain had merely shrugged his shoulders, but she'd felt his apparent indifference was not without pain. One day when the time was right she would learn more about the estrangement between him and his father, but for the present time she'd just have to accept that it existed.

Tearing her mind away from the problem, she smiled at Martine. 'I was very much hoping his sister would come, but she's expecting a baby any week now and the airline refuse to fly her. I spoke to her on the phone though, and she sounded really thrilled for both of us. She told me she was prepared to travel by ferry, but it seems her husband, Gerard, won't hear of it.'

'Here...' Martine topped up Alex's glass. 'We'll have to finish the bottle between us; it'll only go flat if we don't.'

'Why not?' Alex sipped her drink, feeling the tension unwind from her muscles. 'At least I managed to arrange not to go into work today, but poor Alain's been coping masterfully with business affairs and sorting out the problems of arranging a wedding at short notice.'

'Did you make any arrangements about the flat with Lindy?' Martine sipped her own drink. 'If there's anything I can do for you——'

'Yes, I did and you can!' Alex answered both questions at once. 'As I suspected, Lindy has decided to throw her lot in with this Texan she's met and has asked for a permanent transfer to the States, so the flat can be put back on the market. I've already spoken to an agent about it, but I'd be eternally grateful if I could leave a few things with you for a while—like my LPs and tapes and my collection of Limoges jugs. When I'm settled in Paris I'll arrange for them to be shipped over.'

'Yes, of course, anything!' Martine agreed happily. 'I'm very flattered you're marrying one of my countrymen. I just hope you'll both be as happy as Tony and I are!' The smile died from her face, leaving it strained and drawn, as her voice softened. 'You know, all that's missing from our happiness is a baby, Alex. I know many childless couples are perfectly content, but I just feel there's this awful gap in our lives...' Tears filled her eyes and brimmed over. 'Oh, do forgive me for crying at a time when I should be celebrating, but I'm so full of suspense. I can't wait to go back into hospital and have this operation. The surgeon has such very high hopes of putting things right, and he's promised to fit me in at the earliest possible opportunity...' She stopped speaking to dab at her eyes with a tissue.

'Oh, darling Martine...' Alex put her arm round the other girl's shoulders and hugged her, wanting to comfort her but hesitant of sounding too confident in case there was further disappointment ahead for her friend. 'I promise to remember you and Tony in my prayers every night!'

'You know, I'm going to miss you dreadfully,' still tearful, Martine clutched at Alex's shoulder, 'and I know Tony will do as well.' A small smile lit her face. 'He calls you a "real brick", you know. It doesn't sound very complimentary to me. I've always thought of bricks as being thick and red, but he assures me in English it's a compliment!'

'One of the nicest he could pay me!' Alex agreed with a grin, as she glanced at her watch. 'Heavens, Martine, I'll have to fly. I didn't realise how late it was getting. I'm meeting Alain in town for dinner and a resumé of all the day's happenings.'

'Enjoy yourself, then,' Martine instructed her amiably. 'And if there's a lull in the conversation give him a kiss from me and tell him I look forward to dancing at his wedding.'

Some two hours later, still in a daze which had affected her all day, Alex handed the menu back across the table of the elegant restaurant Alain had chosen for their evening meal.

'You choose for me.'

'All right.' He accepted her challenge with total confidence. 'How about mushrooms à la Greque, followed by duckling with pineapple, mangetout and Parisienne potatoes, and for dessert iced zabaglione?'

'Lovely.' Alex relaxed in her chair in anticipation of the feast to come. 'You seem to know my tastes very well. Are we having wine?'

A dark eyebrow lifted in feigned astonishment. 'You dare to ask a Frenchman that? How do you feel about a good claret?'

'Rather devastated, to be honest,' she admitted. 'I've only recently finished off a bottle of champagne with one of my friends.'

'Then you'll feel nice and mellow when I take you back to my apartment when we've finished eating. I've bought a new cassette tape I think you'll enjoy listening to.'

The way he was looking at her made it impossible for Alex to meet his gaze with any hope of retaining her cool air of detachment, as a warm shiver of awareness crept up her spine in response to the expression of his golden eyes.

'You will come back with me, won't you, Alex?'

The message in his dark, intense scrutiny was unmistakable as it roamed across her face, following the line of her neck to rest momentarily on the delicate embroidery of the blue blouse she wore, before returning to her eyes.

The only thing she'd ever saved herself for was love, and love was what she felt in every fibre of her being for the man whose wife she'd agreed to become. Still trying to come to terms with an emotion which had lifted her appreciation of life and all its offerings far more than the best vintage champagne could ever have done, she leaned across the table towards him. 'You don't have to be coy, *chéri*. If you want to take me back to your apartment to make love to me, just say so,' she teased, speaking softly, taking immense pleasure as his expressive face betrayed him utterly.

The next moment she was gasping as, moving with the speed of lightning, he reached across the table to seize her hand, drawing her forward further still until her face was only a few inches from his own.

'I want to take you back to my apartment and make love to you!' It was barely a breath from half-parted lips, yet it sent the blood singing through her veins as he devoured her with a glinting humour from beneath his thick lashes. 'Now what do you say, my love, hmm?'

Recovering quickly, she gave him a quick, enchanting smile. 'I say—I hope the service here is quick.'

For one brief second she wondered if he was going to forget propriety to such a degree that he would actually kiss her then and there. Whether it was the ingrained habits of a lifetime or the opportune arrival of the waiter which broke the spell between them, she would never know.

Unfolding the linen napkin across her skirt, Alex could only be glad that for whatever the reason she hadn't been lured into falling from social grace in a public place. Her inhibitions were too rigid to have allowed her to enjoy the experience. Once in Alain's apartment, alone with the man she loved and was going to marry...there would be no inhibitions...

As one course followed another Alain brought her up to date with the events with which he'd been dealing.

'Fortunately, I've got this friend at the French Embassy and he's been most helpful,' he confided. 'It's quite simple for me to provide all the necessary documentation in time for the date we've chosen, and there's no problem about fixing the time for late afternoon as we agreed. That way we can invite your friends from the London office without disrupting the bank's operation too much!' He paused to sip his wine. 'I've also managed to reserve one of the reception suites at the Park Hotel for a buffet-style meal afterwards. I've told them we'll notify them of numbers in a few days' time.'

'I can hardly believe it's all happening!' Alex shook her blonde head wonderingly. 'This time last week if anyone had told me you were my future husband I would have called them mad!'

'Second thoughts, Alex?' It was a stranger's face regarding her, suddenly cold and remote, causing a faint cold shiver of apprehension to tease her backbone.

'No, no, of course not!' she hastened to reassure him, her voice a little indignant. 'I never go back on my word.'

'I'm glad,' he told her simply but the smile that touched his lips left his eyes unmoved. Hard and cool as polished amber, they rested speculatively on her face. 'The fact is I have a rather reactionary view of marriage, and perhaps it's just as well you understand how I feel before we go through the ceremony.'

'Please——' She lifted a hand towards him inviting him to continue, her face growing serious and a faint *frisson* of warning tensing her posture as she recognised he was in deadly earnest.

'I don't have any strong religious persuasions, Alex, which is why I'm perfectly happy to marry in a register office, but I still regard it as a binding contract—a bargain between two people that is irrevocable, come what may.'

'Yes, yes, I agree.' She looked anxiously at his stern face, a tremor of disquiet still plaguing her. 'Are you saying you doubt my sincerity, Alain?'

It was the signal for him to tell her that he loved and trusted her, but he didn't. Instead he continued quietly, 'Alex, not every story ends with the hero and heroine living happily ever after. There has to be room for compromise. It's like a business. It's impossible to build it into a thriving concern unless one can depend on its stability—and especially where there are children, young children, their needs must come first, even if it means sacrifice, subjugating one's own needs and desires. After all, adults go into liaisons voluntarily, knowing what they're taking on. In so many cases children become victims of their parents' selfishness and vanity. I wouldn't want that to happen to any son or daughter of mine.'

'Neither would I.' Shocked and disturbed, she met his eyes, her own misting a little at the thought of conceiving a child by this man who was capable of changing from intimate companion to stranger in the blink of an eye. 'I'm not the kind of woman to throw tantrums at the slightest provocation, or go into sullen silences. And I've never reneged on a bargain yet.' Her chin lifted a little higher as she challenged him. 'Actually you're in a better position than most to know the extent of my integrity— or haven't you run my name through the computer yet?' She swallowed unhappily, as she realised she was provoking a quarrel, but the pain his doubt had caused her couldn't be denied. With an effort she kept her voice low and well-modulated. 'If you've got those kind of doubts about my character, perhaps we should wait a little longer before going ahead with our plans——?'

'That's not what I'm saying!' he interrupted her harshly. 'Dear lord, Alex! I'm moving heaven and earth to get things progressing quickly and smoothly. I just want you to know the score. You know what I'm offering you. If you decide to take it then that decision's final. I'd never make it easy for you to leave me!'

'You're right, *chéri*.' Conscious of his distress, she forgot her own hurt, her soft voice relieving the tension from the atmosphere. 'You *are* reactionary—but then, so am I, and to be honest with you I should be very disappointed if I thought you would make it easy for me to leave you—and for my part...'

'Yes?' The strain had left his face and Alex was filled with a deep feminine satisfaction that she had the power to defuse a potentially dangerous build-up of emotion.

She gave the little Gallic shrug which Martine used so effectively, pursing her lips and spreading her fingers expressively. 'For my part, Monsieur du Gard, if you tried to escape from me, I'd—I'd tie you to the bedpost!'

She watched his eyes darken appreciatively as a long dimple deepened in his cheek, turning him once more into a man who showed he could be tender beneath the outer toughness. 'You must be psychic, my love. How did you guess I've ordered a four-poster for our Paris house?'

She guessed he was teasing, experiencing a sense of relief that a perilous moment had passed. Presumably he'd been thinking of his own childhood earlier. She knew so little about it, only that it must have been painful, leaving behind scars the sensitivity of which she could only guess at. In time she would find out—if he wanted to tell her and if the telling gave him comfort. She envisaged lying in bed with him, cradling his head against her breast, stroking his sable hair, listening...comforting...reassuring. In time giving him back his faith in human nature as she bore, gave birth to and loved his children...

'I'm sorry?' She'd been so lost in her romantic dreams she'd missed what he'd just said, only being aware that he was regarding her with raised eyebrows, awaiting her answer.

'The honeymoon,' he repeated patiently. 'I was saying that you might want to tie me to the bedpost sooner than you anticipated. There's one hell of a storm brewing at the moment in the financial take-over section and I really can't afford to disappear to the Caribbean at this stage of the proceedings.'

'Oh, Alain!' She smothered a laugh, recalling the disdain on his face that morning when he'd overheard what she'd supposedly required from a potential husband. 'You think that matters?' Couldn't he sense that wherever *he* was—that was fine with her! 'I'd settle for the North Pole!' she told him, making her point as forcefully as possible. Her dislike of snow and ice was legendary in the office!

'Sorry, Alex,' he said, pretending dismay. 'That's too many jet hours away as well. As a matter of fact I thought we could spend our wedding night in London, stay in Paris while I report to head office and tidy up a few things, and then make tracks for my villa in Corsica. It's not St Lucia, but it has a charm of its own.'

'Tell me about it,' she invited eagerly, as their dessert plates were removed to be replaced with *demi-tasses* of fragrant coffee. Her quick perception had seen the nostalgia in his eyes, caught a hint of defensiveness as he'd mentioned the island.

CHAPTER SEVEN

'YOU may not find it a very exciting location.' Again the diffidence warned Alex to tread wearily, so she contented herself with nodding encouragingly for Alain to continue. 'It's built on the hills about a kilometre behind a small fishing village where life hasn't changed since Napoleon was a boy. But beyond the small harbour there's a curving scimitar of sand which stretches for eight hundred metres—and the sea is turquoise and scintillates like a precious gem beneath a jeweller's light.' His gaze slid over her expectant face. 'But there's only a village shop and a small bistro. No night life, no fancy food or international cooking, no hotels or discos.'

'It sounds marvellous!' Alex was astounded that he should even suspect she would look with disfavour on such a paradise. 'I'm certain I shall love it, however primitive it is!'

Across the table from her Alain laughed at her outraged expression. 'Relax, *ma colombe*, the villa's not primitive—just the setting.' His eyes narrowed thoughtfully. 'You wouldn't be bored without entertainment?'

On her honeymoon? She bit back the words. Alain was a mature man, confident and controlled. Of course they wouldn't spend every hour of every day making love! That was a seaside postcard concept of a honeymoon. There would be exciting hours of building tension, intellectual and verbal foreplay culminating in a marvellous explosion of their feelings for each other! Alain was the experienced one. He would lead her, tutor her...and she would be a willing and adept pupil.

Together they would discover what pleased the other, learning each other's rhythms... elegantly, with sophistication... Colour suffused her face as her body responded to her own thoughts. Conscious of Alain's amused gaze fixed on her flushed face she answered as nonchalantly as she could, 'Not if I can swim and sunbathe and walk...'

'And how about the evenings—what will you do with your time then?' His dark eyebrows rose interrogatively.

'Well...' If it was an invitation to make verbal love to him across the table she wouldn't rise to the bait. Already her wayward thoughts had speeded up her metabolic system to an uncomfortable rate. 'I—I shall sit on the terrace... it has a terrace?' And as he nodded, 'And watch the moon rise and listen to the cicadas and drink in the perfume of the *maquis*!' She paused then added wistfully, 'Can you smell the *maquis* from the villa?'

'Yes, oh, yes.' His smile was reminiscent, soft with affection. 'You can smell the *maquis* in Corsica the moment you step off the plane. Other Mediterranean islands have a similar heavy scent from their wild plants, but there's nothing quite like *la Corse*. From the villa it's inescapable, because the hills behind it are thick with vegetation.'

Vitally aware she was sharing something which was very close to his heart she said softly, 'It's a very special place for you, isn't it, Alain?'

For a moment she thought he wasn't going to answer her, as if somehow by admitting his affection he would admit an area of pregnability in his personality. Then he said quietly, 'Yes, it is. When I was a child we used to spend part of the summer there—my father, Giselle, the woman who looked after us and me. I found it an enchanted world, a place of endless summer...' He cleared his throat abruptly, signalling to the waiter to present the bill. 'Are you ready to leave, *chérie*?'

'Yes.' Alex nodded to augment her agreement, allowing the waiter to help her on with her jacket as Alain handed over his Gold credit card.

Sinking back into the comfortable upholstery of his Jaguar, which had been brought round to the front door of the restaurant to await them, she was content to sit in silence as they drove through the city streets.

As she entered the luxury Barbican apartment the bank had leased for him, she gained a quick impression of dark carpets and light walls, elegant table lamps and soft, luxurious furniture before Alain turned towards her, gathering her to his body with urgent, demanding hands, pulling her into his arms, taking her mouth in a long, deep, erotic kiss that made her go weak-kneed.

Blissfully she raised her hands to caress his neck, entwining her fingers in the thick sable hair, discovering it to be surprisingly fine and silky, her last lingering doubts about his bewildering outburst fading as she sensed the cogent response of his finely tuned body. When he turned her gently, pushing her back against his left arm, dropping his right hand to find the point where her blouse entered the waistband of her flared skirt, sliding smoothly beneath it, murmuring inarticulately as he stroked the warm, satin nakedness of her skin, she almost purred with pleasure.

'Wait...' he muttered huskily, loosing her for a moment to discard his jacket and tie unceremoniously over the arm of a chair before reaching again for her, discovering the narrow lace of her bra, sliding his fingers beneath it while she gasped as her sensitised skin responded as if stirred by electrodes to his magic.

His long-sleeved, beautifully cut, body-hugging shirt proved no barrier to Alex's slim hand, the buttons slipping with surprising ease from their holes as her fingers crept inside to touch the astonishing smoothness of his lightly tanned chest. Pressing the hollow of her hand over the deep, slow beat of his heart, she sighed with delight. She'd never doubted the rightness of her decision—but if she had... Well, this incredible glow which held her in its thrall would be enough to persuade her that their meeting had been ordained in heaven... their future planned by some divine benevolence...

She was dazed with sensuous enjoyment and her breath came fast and shallow as Alain's deft fingers stroked and cajoled her eager breasts to an aching response.

'Alex, *mon chéri*...' The deep timbre of his voice shook as he took her hand from his heart, kissing the palm before replacing it on the outside of his clothing at waist-level. Instantly she knew his need, reassuring him with her touch, feeling a deep joy that it was she who was able to awaken his beautiful, vital male body to this instinctive surge of desire.

'A-a-h...' He buried his face in the hollow between her cheek and shoulder, shuddering deeply. 'Are you going to make me wait until our wedding night?' he asked hoarsely. 'Because if you are I think we'd better forget about the music and you'd better leave now while you still can.'

Locked in his arms, clinging to him for support, Alex gave a breathless little laugh, immensely flattered he wasn't taking her compliance for granted. 'What makes you think I still can anyway?' she asked sweetly.

His slow, sweet sigh of satisfaction and relief registered on her ears a split second before the sharp electronic bleep of the telephone.

'Hell and damnation!' He choked the oath, his hands tightening on her shoulders. 'Let it ring!'

'No.' She pushed at his chest, her control marginally less shattered. 'You'll have to answer it. Just get rid of whoever it is quickly!'

Muttering to himself, Alain released her, taking quick, angry strides to the lobby. Tucking her blouse back inside her skirt in a purely reflex action, her hands trembling, Alex prayed it was a wrong number. When he didn't return immediately she knew her prayers had been ignored.

By the time he strode back into the room, his face white and taut, the fury of his darkened eyes a fearful power between them, she was resigned to the fact their love was not to be consummated that night.

'Zurich!' he spat out. 'I have to fly to Zurich of all places—and now of all times! Alex, listen...' He dropped to his knees beside the armchair where she'd seated herself in his absence. 'I tried my damnedest to get out of it, but they're relying on me. There's been one hell of a mix-up in Paris and Dubois, the bank's president, insists I'm the only man who can sort it out with our branch in Zurich. They've been trying to get me since six this evening.' His breath exhaled in heavy exasperation. 'They've even got a plane standing by at Gatwick now.'

He was shaking, whether from frustrated passion or anger Alex couldn't determine, her own feelings too mixed to allow her to judge impartially. '*Dieu!* How can I ask you to forgive me?' His jaw clenched, the muscles of his cheek held rigidly, and a deadly temper flared on his set face.

'Very easily.' Masking her own disappointment, Alex forced herself to speak easily. 'If I'm to marry such an incredibly important man, the sooner I get used to his lifestyle, the better.'

When his mouth released hers, warm and swollen from the loving assault he imposed on it, she struggled to keep her voice from shaking. 'When will you be coming back, darling?'

'In time for our wedding, you can be assured,' he retorted grimly. 'Nothing and nobody will keep me from that—and I'll phone you every night to see how you are and to discuss arrangements. Alex?' For a man so sure of himself and his power, his deep voice held an element of uncertainty to her sensitive ears. 'You won't change your mind—will you?'

'No—of course not.' It had taken her twenty-four years to find what she wanted. She meant to hold on to it, hell, high water or Zurich. Her own frustration must have been as great as his, but at that moment she knew she was the one with the greater control. 'Which room is the bedroom?' she asked lightly, smiling slightly at the piquancy of the question. 'I'll help you pack.'

He left for Gatwick while she was still waiting for the arrival of the taxi he'd ordered to take her back to her own flat. Placing the spare key he'd given her in her purse, she tried to come to terms with her sense of anti-climax. Was it better this way? Or would the parting have been less painful if they'd had the time to become lovers? A long time later she would realise that, if that phone call had been delayed for an hour, the whole pattern of the coming weeks might have been changed.

Ten days later when the doorbell of her flat rang with impatient insistence, Alex hurried to answer it. A slim, smiling Martine stepped over the threshold.

'Oh, Alex—you look fabulous!' Her appreciative gaze absorbed the elegant lines of the pink-champagne-coloured silk dress and jacket Alex wore, purchased specially for her wedding, the shoulder-line of the jacket fashionably padded, the peplum nipped in at her small waist and softly fluted over her neat hips. The dress beneath was sleeveless, cut high in the neck but dipping intriguingly at the back to give a hint of finely moulded shoulder-blades before flaring into a stylish tulip shape at just below knee-level.

To be honest, she still felt a little guilty at its cost, consoling herself with the fact that she just hadn't had the time to put into practice her own dressmaking skills. Besides, it was an outfit that would see the light of day many more times than a traditional wedding dress would, so there was some justification in having taken her custom to Harvey Nichols, she supposed, and choosing one of the top ten British designers.

Alain had intimated in one of their frantic phone conversations that he didn't want her to spare any expense, telling her he would settle all bills she incurred. Not that she would allow him to pay for this outfit. For reasons which weren't entirely clear to herself she wanted to buy her own trousseau. Probably a last display of independence, she accorded ruefully, uncertain how she would settle down to a life of domesticity rather than business. If only she and Alain had had more time to discuss the future, although she doubted if he'd seriously demur against her finding a pleasing occupation...

'Tony's just parking,' Martine explained, breaking into her thoughts. 'I take it the bridegroom's safely back in England?'

'Just!' Alex reassured her with a grimace. 'He flew back last night and phoned me first thing this morning to let me know I wasn't going to be left waiting at the register office.'

Martine shook her dark head in mock despair. 'Men!' Her compassionate glance encompassed Alex's rather strained expression. 'Why don't you go and sit down

while I make you a cup of coffee to steady your nerves?'
she suggested.

'Thanks, I'd appreciate that.' It wasn't until she
actually subsided in an armchair that Alex realised how
tense she was. Not surprising really. The days had passed
in a mass of activity culminating in an efficiently
arranged ceremony and reception for forty-six people.
Or, at least, that was what she was depending on! True
to his word, Alain had telephoned her regularly, checking
on progress and doing everything he could to facilitate
matters. Zoe, his temporary secretary at the bank's
London headquarters, had proved an invaluable ally too.
Gratefully accepting the coffee from Martine, Alex
sighed. In any case, it was too late to worry now. In half
an hour she would be Madame Alain Du Gard with all
the responsibilities and pleasures that title conjured up.
Unexpectedly she shivered.

'Tony says we should be leaving soon.' Martine eyed
her speculatively. 'Are you cold or is it just nerves, Alex?
Or . . . have you had a change of heart? It's not too late,
you know, right up to the time you make the contract.'

'What? Oh . . .' She hugged her arms across her breast,
feeling the goose-flesh beneath the exquisite Chinese silk.
'What a thing to say to me!' She forced herself to utter
a laugh. 'I guess I was just having a few last thoughts
as a single girl.'

'But no regrets, hmm?'

'Of course not!' This time her voice was more confident. Of course she didn't have regrets. She might not
have known Alain for a long time, but she loved him.
There was no other way to explain the way he made her
feel, the loneliness and emptiness she had experienced
these past few days, the way her whole body had thrilled
just to hear his voice on the phone. And he loved her
too! Why else would he have asked her to become his

wife? She was everything he wanted, wasn't she? Physically attractive, well-bred and never owned by another man—besides which they knew enough about each other to want to spend the remainder of their lives discovering the rest. It was just that she'd expected to share some time with him before the ceremony...

'Then we may as well make a start—unless you deliberately want to keep Alain waiting?' Martine, looking vibrantly attractive in a scarlet coat and matching pillbox hat, cast her a wicked grin. 'I believe it's traditional?'

'Oh, no, I couldn't possibly!' Shocked, Alex rose to her feet.

'Because he might be angry or because he might get cold feet himself?' Dark eyes glimmered with fun at Alex's outraged expression.

'Because it would be too cruel,' she returned firmly, walking to the table and picking up a wide-brimmed, caramel-coloured fine straw hat, arranging it at a slight angle on her pretty head. 'How does that look?'

'Like a painting by Gainsborough,' Martine approved. 'I can't wait to see the bridegroom's face when he sees you.' She handed Alex the gloves and handbag which matched the suit. 'All the luck in the world, darling!' Bestowing a quick hug round her friend's shoulders, Martine walked swiftly to the door. 'This is it, then. Operation Wedding Day.'

Several hours later, flushed with vintage champagne, happiness lending her an almost ethereal glow, Alex danced in the arms of her husband. Slim and beautiful, she trembled in his embrace, the bare skin of her back reacting feverishly to the touch of his hand as it rested lightly against it. Oddly, she could scarcely remember the ceremony itself, only that it had apparently proceeded without a hitch, both she and Alain had made the correct responses at the correct time, and the guests had all arrived well and happy and appeared to be enjoying themselves.

There had been no formal speeches, Alain contenting himself with welcoming the guests on behalf of himself and his wife and inviting them to eat, drink and dance to their hearts' content. There'd been animated conversations with people she hadn't seen for months, friendly teasing from Simone and Zoe, and a delighted reunion with Dudley and Liz as well as introductions to other acquaintances of Alain's whom she hadn't previously met. Now, secure in his arms, she felt a dangerous elation thrumming through her system.

'Like Eliza Dolittle, I think I could dance all night,' she declared, tilting her head back the better to look into his eyes, her blonde hair swirling its silken tendrils against her shoulders.

'And I was considering leaving after this dance,' he murmured, his mouth a mere fraction away from her ear as he closed the distance between them.

'Already?' She forced her lovely mouth into a pout, teasing him, guessing he was anticipating the further recreation the evening still had to offer them. 'I haven't been dancing for ages and I'm enjoying myself! Besides, I know Simone would die happy if you'd take her in your arms!'

'*D'accord, mon ange.*' He smiled at her lazily, indulgently, but there was a sharpness behind the complaisancy of his gaze which offered her an indeterminate warning. 'How refreshing it is not to have to pander to a jealous woman. I will certainly oblige the enchanting Simone since it's your wish.' He shot back the cuff of his beautifully tailored silver-grey suit, glancing at his watch. 'Another half an hour, then, after which I'm sure our guests will consider our duty done and be only too happy to speed us on our way.'

As the music stopped he led her back towards the buffet table still amply covered despite the inroads already made on it. Nibbling on a canapé, she watched his steady progress across the large room to where Simone stood in animated conversation with a small group of other guests. A man who walked with pride and authority in every stride, she reflected, feeling a strange restlessness grip her.

Madame du Gard... She lowered her gaze to stare down at the wide, chased gold ring which graced her finger. Sadly she had had to choose it by herself in Alain's enforced absence. Her thoughts began to run on. If only her parents and Jamie had been here with her. Without them it was almost as if she were dreaming, could awaken at any moment and find her handsome banker prince only a figment of her imagination, the excitement and euphoria of the past ten days exposed as a delirium.

To her absolute horror she felt tears filling her eyes as she experienced a choking misery. Had she acted recklessly? What did she know of Alain's life in France? Would she fit in with his lifestyle? Suppose she had made a mistake? She was fully adult, independent, able to make her own decisions but, oh, if only her family could have been here with her today...

Appalled at the passage of her thoughts and the disastrous result they were having, she fumbled in her bag for a tissue, dabbing at her eyes, trying to stem the tears without damaging her make-up. Dear lord—please let no one see her like this!

'Alex! Whatever's wrong?' A comforting arm hugged her as Tony's light voice, deepened with concern, addressed her in a soft undertone.

'Ah, Tony...thank heavens it's you.' She dabbed again at the recalcitrant tears. 'I mustn't let anyone see me like this, they'll think Alain's been coming the heavy husband!' She forced a watery smile.

'Are you sure he hasn't?' A certain grimness hardened his tone. 'Because——'

'Because—nothing, Tony!' But she was glad of his protection. 'I just need to get out of here for a few moments. It's just that I'm a bit overwrought and I got to thinking about Mum and Dad and wishing they were here...and now I can't seem to stop crying. Please don't let Alain know!'

'If that's all, then...' He looked at her doubtfully, then, reassured by her nod, made a quick decision. 'There's a small private bar the other side of this wall. I found it by mistake when I was looking for the loo. There are mirrors in there as well, and it'll save you running the gauntlet by having to walk the entire length of this room to reach the sanctuary of the cloakroom. Here, this way.' He took charge, ushering her discreetly through the half-hidden door.

'That's better!' Gratefully she slid into one of the velvet-covered bench seats discreetly positioned in pairs within wooden partitions. Relieved of the strain of becoming the cynosure of all eyes, she allowed her tears to flow freely for a few seconds before giving Tony an apologetic smile. 'I can't think what came over me. I'm not usually so emotional, as you know.'

'But then you don't usually fall in love and get married all within the space of a couple of weeks,' Tony told her philosophically. 'Heavens, Alex! You've been driving yourself pretty hard. It's only to be expected you'd have a reaction.'

'I guess so.' Certainly she felt a lot better now, hazarding that the panic of being seen weeping by the guests had exacerbated a tiny moment of regret into a storm out of all proportion. 'Anyway, I feel fine now. I'll just tidy up my face and we can go back before anyone misses us.' She turned half sideways to where a copper mirror on the wall reflected the table and its occupants, carefully removing slight smudges of mascara from her lower lids, while Tony regarded her with tender affection.

'I'll never forget the weeks you spent with me while Martine was in hospital.'

'Neither will I!' She touched his hand with the comradeship of long standing, her smile denying the ruefulness of her expression.

'I didn't let you have much sleep,' he agreed contritely.

'No, you didn't! But it was worth it!' She would have gone without sleep entirely if necessary, so that Martine could stay in hospital without worrying about her husband, and Tony's bouts of midnight depression and self-immolation hadn't been too difficult to contend with.

She glanced at his sensitive face, knowing that he was much more emotionally stable than he had been. If only he didn't allow himself to become over-confident about Martine's operation. An unexpected disappointment might destroy his new-found strength and in such tragic circumstances Martine would need durable support.

'Tony...' She broke the small silence. 'You do realise that it's not absolutely certain about the baby, don't you?'

To her relief, he nodded. 'The tests weren't totally conclusive, but the odds are definitely in favour of pregnancy, aren't they? In any case, I know we've made the right decision to go ahead as we agreed. If there's a baby it's going to get a really good start in life—and if not...' He shrugged his shoulders philosophically. 'If not, no great damage will have been done.'

'Yes, you're right,' Alex agreed soberly. 'You know, I want this baby as much as you do.'

'Bless you...' He acknowledged her concern, touching her arm with grateful fingers. 'These last few weeks have been hell for both of us, but this morning——' He broke off in mid-sentence, producing a card from his pocket and pushing it across the table. With astonishment Alex identified a hospital admission card. So they'd found Martine a bed already!

'Does Martine know?' Puzzled because her friend hadn't even hinted at the good news, she frowned questioningly at Tony.

'No, she doesn't.' He shook his head. 'I thought it best to keep it from her until after your wedding. You know how she is...'

Yes, she knew. Volatile and emotional, desperately in love with her husband and equally desperate to bear his child. Tony was right. Alone in the privacy of their own house where they could mutually express their hopes and fears in their own time—that was where the news should be broken. Alex's respect for Tony increased with the knowledge of his reticence.

'You're quite a guy, Mr Gibson. I'm going to miss you.' Her admiration shone clear and uncomplicated for the man he'd become.

'And I you—quite dreadfully, Alex,' he admitted, making no attempt to hide his regret. 'You were always there when I needed you and I can't get used to the idea you'll be living in France from now on.'

'I'll write,' she promised. 'Regular news letters, and I expect to hear from you too!'

'And if there's a baby?' All his hopes for the future were in the question and on his pleasant face. Alex squeezed his arm. 'Then we'll meet at the christening, I promise you.'

'What more can I ask?' He surveyed her critically.
'You look as beautiful as ever, Alex. Ready to go back
and face the crowd?'

'Quite ready,' she said firmly. 'And thanks for the face-
saving action.'

'Any time, Alex.' He stood back to allow her to
precede him to the door. 'Any time, anywhere you need
help, Martine and I will always be there for you. You
only have to ask.'

'I hope I shan't have to, but thanks, Tony.'

She allowed him to take her in his arms and ease her
from the quiet room into the main reception-room,
joining the dancers as they encircled the floor.

She had Alain now as her defender and champion,
her Sir Lancelot du Lac. *His* strong arms would protect
her; *his* name would give her social standing and respect.
His love would encompass her and give her future life
a marvellous magic. *His* presence in her life would protect
her from all evil. That was what love was all about, and
tonight when they consummated their mutual passion
she would become invulnerable. The thought gave her
so much anticipatory pleasure that she smiled up into
her partner's face, her eyes shining with a deep joy, her
soft skin flushed to a peach-blossom beauty.

'Are you ready to leave yet?' It was several partners
later when Alain claimed her attention by catching her
firmly by the arm, surprising her with the hint of
annoyance which sharpened the tone of his question.

Glancing guiltily at the small cocktail watch which
adorned her left wrist, Alex saw that it was close on ten
o'clock. Nearly an hour had passed since the last time
she'd spoken to him.

'I'm sorry, darling.' She blazed a smile at him com-
pounded of love and apology. 'I had no idea how late
it was getting. Yes, of course, I'm ready.'

'Good!' He didn't return her smile, leaving her feeling a pang of guilt. Surely he would understand that it was no reluctance to be alone with him that had kept her dancing, only a heady euphoria of which he was the key progenitor? But there was nothing on his set face to affirm her hope. Still, if his male ego had been wounded she would find a suitable balm to soothe it as soon as they gained the privacy of his apartment. She lowered her gaze, unwilling for him to discern the secret seductive smile that twitched the corners of her mouth.

Sitting silently beside him in the Jaguar as he drove steadily towards their destination, she was content to relax, closing her eyes and enjoying the smooth movement of the car and his heady presence beside her.

'There are a few things I have to do before I leave London.' They were the first words he'd spoken to her since leaving the hotel, as he ushered her through the front door of his apartment. 'So you'll forgive me if I seem to neglect you.' It was a statement rather than a question as he moved away from her to retrieve a large briefcase from its place beside an imposing bureau. 'You know your way around, so I'm sure you can amuse yourself while I'm working.'

'Of course I can.' Adroitly Alex masked her disappointment. How selfish she'd been to expect him to take her into his arms and make passionate love to her the instant they stepped over the threshold. Hadn't she already acknowledged to them both the need for her to become used to the demands his career made on him? She'd been stupid as well as conceited to imagine that his urgency to leave the hotel had been solely on her account. 'Did you have a bad time at Zurich?' she asked sympathetically.

'Complicated,' he returned tersely, opening the briefcase and tipping out several folders, selecting one and beginning to scan its contents with impatient eyes.

Clearly not the time to ask for confidences or indulge in conversation. Alex sighed lightly. Far better to leave him to his own devices. The sooner he started, the sooner he'd finish. The last thing he'd want now was for her to play the loving seductress. Discretion would be her middle name!

'In that case, I think I'll get ready for bed,' she told him pleasantly. 'I'll see you later.'

'Mmm.' It was no more than a polite acknowledgement that she'd spoken.

Ah, well, she thought with resignation, she'd take advantage of the situation to perform a long, luxurious *toilette*, perhaps even indulge in the fantasy that she was a concubine preparing herself for the favours of her master! Quietly she left the room with one last lingering look at Alain's dark head, successfully restraining her instinct to run her fingers through his thick hair and place a promising kiss on the nape of his neck where its waywardness had been beautifully tamed by some Swiss *coiffeur*.

As he'd said, the layout of the apartment was no mystery to her. Having been left his spare key, she'd visited the premises several times in his absence to deal with matters concerning the wedding ceremony and also to leave her case packed with her trousseau ready for Paris and Corsica.

After enjoying a leisurely bath, during which she half hoped Alain wouldn't be able to concentrate on his business to the exclusion of interrupting her, she anointed herself with perfumed body foam before putting on the apricot silk and lace nightdress which had been Martine's personal gift to her, ordered and delivered direct from

Galeries Lafayette in Paris—a confection of mouth-watering lusciousness which, to her careful appraisal, appeared to turn her normal slim curves into a sensual voluptuousness.

Resisting the impulse to disturb Alain, she climbed into the double bed. How fortuitous it was that the Banque de Varcennes recognised that its male employees might prefer the greater space and luxury of a large bed. Or, perhaps, she accorded realistically, they merely accepted that directors abroad might not always wish to sleep alone!

There were magazines on the bedside table, but it seemed the long day was already beginning to take its toll of her. Alex yawned, deciding to take a refreshing catnap before her bridegroom joined her.

CHAPTER EIGHT

ALEX awakened with a start some time later, automatically reaching out a hand to find herself still the sole occupant of the bed. Turning her head, she made out the time on the illuminated clock at her side. Two o'clock! Surely Alain couldn't still be working? Thrusting back thé soft duvet, she swung her legs out of bed, running her fingers through her hair, scrunching it into some order before making for the door. He must have fallen asleep over his papers. After all, it had been a gruelling ten days for him. Worse than for her because he'd borne the brunt of a demanding job.

'Alain?' She blinked as the light of the room struck her large-pupilled eyes and she attempted to focus on the figure sprawled in one of the armchairs, one long leg hooked negligently over the side of it, a sheaf of papers in one hand. 'You're not still working?'

He didn't answer immediately, but she was conscious of his steady gaze travelling over the picture she presented clinging to the door-lintel, the apricot satin outlining every curve and hollow of her nubile form.

'It's a question of priorities, *ma chère*.' His eyes dwelt on her face, the lids still heavy from sleep, her blonde hair tousled as if by a lover's fingers, her mouth softly pink against her clear, un-made-up complexion. 'You have to remember that it's my work that's going to provide you with the designer wardrobe, the Italian sports car and the Caribbean holidays.'

'Don't tease me,' she said plaintively, her heart aching, because her pupils had adjusted to the light and she could

see how tautly his skin seemed to stretch across the bones
of his face. 'Come to bed, Alain. Can't the rest of it
wait?'

'Is that what you want?' His golden eyes invited her
to confirm her desire. Still bemused from prolonged
sleep, she thought she detected something dark and
dangerous lurking behind the mask of admiring
masculinity.

'Do you doubt it?' She advanced towards him, moving
sinuously, her body warm and already wanton beneath
the caressing folds of silk, remembering the last time she
had graced his lap wearing nothing but the silken art of
a couturier. Then she had been wary of the rampant male
predator clothed in the respectability of heritage and
profession—now he was her husband and there was no
need for apprehension.

As she came within arm's reach of him Alain pulled
her down into the chair, mimicking the incident she
recalled so clearly, only this time his hands moved with
the sureness of ownership, taking without asking,
pushing the silken folds of the nightdress away from her
shoulders, baring her breasts with a passion bordering
on emotional frenzy. She could feel the shiver that
engulfed him as his hands followed the soft contours of
her breasts, his breath shuddering through half-parted
lips as she sought to catch his face between her palms.

It was as if he was racked by some inner pain as his
graceful, capable hands moved over her pale skin with
a tenderness and sensitivity at odds with the unsmiling
lines of his countenance. Bewildered by what appeared
to be some inner battle he was fighting, Alex longed to
comfort him, to still the rasping agony of his lungs,
reaching out to return his caresses, her eager hands
moving towards the fine linen of his shirt, determined
to fondle the warm, tanned skin that pulsed beneath its
pristine cover.

Impatiently he brushed her searching fingers aside as if the feel of them offended him. Then, as she froze at his peremptory rejection, his own caresses grew more bold, his urgent fingers pushing the apricot silk further down her body with the ease of unpeeling the fruit itself, seeking to bestow on her the most intimate of caresses with a delicacy of touch that abolished all other thoughts from her mind. It was a solicitous tribute to her femininity, filling her with an extraordinary mindless pleasure that drowned all other feelings.

'Alain...' Flung across his lap, her head resting on his shoulder, her whole being filled with the scent and touch of him, she whispered his name like a caress, aware that he was giving freely, asking nothing in return while he kindled and ignited fires hidden so deep within her she had only half dreamed of their existence. As he lowered his head to catch the perfect tip of one opalescent breast between his lips, she uttered a cry as pleasure bordered on pain, and she realised through the mist of gratification enfolding her that she'd been brought by a master of the art to the brink of something terrifying and wonderful. Poised on the brink of ecstasy, her lips parted, her breath coming in short, fast gasps, she could only await the release that was in Alain's gift.

Unable to formulate the words to beg his mercy, she could only return the mesmeric stare of his topaz, half-shuttered eyes and pray silently for him to break the final cord that held her pinioned to the ground—to break it and let her soar into the fantastic world that she sensed awaited her.

It was then that he left her. Lifting her body to allow him his escape, rising broad-shouldered and tight-hipped, he stood before her looking down at her and she knew with a sickening sense of anticlimax he had no intention of allowing her the satisfaction he intended to deny himself. Not only did he have no objective of making her his wife in anything but name that night, but he was leaving her to find her own laboured way down from the pinnacle to which he'd deliberately raised her.

'I'm sorry to disappoint you,' his voice was harsh and disjointed, the words torn from steel-bound lips ringed with a thin white line, 'but I think it's time we called a halt to this little interlude, enjoyable although it's been. We have an early flight to catch tomorrow and I still have to complete my report.'

Dear heaven! What had she done to deserve this? Suddenly ashamed of her splendid body displaying its vulnerability, she dragged the folds of the nightdress upwards to cover her nudity.

'I'm sorry. I didn't mean to disturb your concentration.' With as much dignity as she could muster she rose to her feet, determined not to let him see how hurt she was by his sudden withdrawal. Perhaps this was another lesson she would have to learn—business always came first. Not that physical love was the only way of expressing affection, only that there had been something deliberately humiliating about the way he had treated her. Difficult to explain, but she was sure she wasn't being over-sensitive... or was she?

'My dear Alex, as I'm sure you know, a woman as lovely as you are is bound to be disturbing to a red-blooded man. The secret of dealing with that kind of disturbance is always to be aware of its danger and in control of its effect. *Tu as compris*?'

No, she didn't understand. Neither did she understand the cruel, thin-lipped smile that stretched the warm contours of his shapely mouth.

'As you were after Epsom?' she asked, unable to refrain from attacking his mocking regard.

'Yes.' He dipped his head in acknowledgement. 'No civilised man has a taste for rape. I happen to believe also that no civilised man should leave himself open to female exploitation. A man's brain should be in his head not beneath his belt, so, *ma chère* Alex, we'll leave the undoubted delight of fully consummating our marriage to a later date when we have the time available so we can both devote ourselves fully to its enjoyment.'

'I'm sure you're right.' Somehow she gathered her senses together. Tomorrow everything would be all right. Today had been fraught with too many anxieties. In truth the early consummation of their marriage was not of primary importance. Hadn't she once read that after the excitement of a wedding-day and the free flowing of alcohol, many couples found themselves unable to make love satisfactorily? Suddenly she thought she understood Alain's reticence! How selfish she'd been... Unlike her, he hadn't even had the respite of a few hours' sleep. Little wonder he didn't want to put himself on trial in case of failure. Although she could have dealt with such an event with compassion and tenderness, she was sensitive enough to realise how devastated a man of Alain's arrogance would have felt.

Rising to her feet, she began to walk towards the bedroom, hesitating after only a few steps and turning to face him. He was watching her, a guarded expression in his half-shuttered eyes. Impulsively she went to him, lifting her arms round his shoulders, raising her lips to his own, kissing him swiftly and warmly. '*Je t'adore*,' she whispered huskily as her mouth left his.

She'd thought to speed away, but he was too fast for her, catching her as she turned, pulling her back into his embrace, taking her mouth with a passionate urgency that had her gasping for breath. She wasn't surprised when his questing tongue forced her lips apart to possess her mouth with a dominance that asked for no co-operation. She felt her knees bend beneath the power of his assault, glad of the strong protection of his arms. As an expression of his feelings for her it was wildly possessive and pregnant with a warning she didn't even begin to comprehend.

When he released her with a curt 'Go to bed, Alex' she walked unsteadily towards the bedroom, aware that he had already returned to his chair and was seemingly re-engrossed in his work. She tumbled on to the mattress, her mouth still warm and throbbing, her body still fighting the clamorous instincts Alain had aroused within its depths and refused or feared himself unable to satisfy.

The morning sunlight struck sparks of reflection from the balcony rail outside the master bedroom as Alex stood against it looking towards the sweep of foliage marking the boundary of the Bois de Boulogne. Alain's apartment on the second floor of a luxury block in a quiet square just off the Rue de Passy would have delighted her if she hadn't been so deeply concerned with the way her relationship with him was developing—or not developing would be the better description, she mused.

Awakening the morning following her wedding-day, she'd been shocked to find the place beside her in bed cold and undisturbed. Irrational fears had sent her speeding out of the room, thankfully quelled by the aroma of freshly brewed coffee, and the appearance of her husband newly shaven and dressed warming up croissants in the kitchen.

In answer to her puzzlement he'd admitted falling to sleep in the chair and not awakening until the first light of morning aroused him. Not typical behaviour of a newly married man, but understandable in the circumstances. She'd chided him good-humouredly, too full of excitement at the prospect of the new life ahead of her to dwell on the matter, or the disturbing events which had preceded his absence from the marital bed.

But last night... that was something different. Alex lifted her face towards the sun, instinctively seeking comfort from its unremitting warmth. The flight to Paris the previous day had been unremarkable and, as she'd stepped into the arrivals lounge of Charles de Gaulle Airport, her normal sunny nature had bounced back and she'd been filled with a glowing happiness and optimism about her new life in Paris.

The day had been busy—filled with new impressions—from being introduced to Alain's efficient and pleasant middle-aged, non-resident housekeeper, Madame Latache, to admiring the layout and furnishings of Alain's home, and exploring the environs of her new location. His being called to head office for a conference hadn't been unexpected, but when he'd phoned to say he wouldn't be back for dinner her disappointment had been a heavy weight to bear.

Uninterested in the programmes on television, she'd spent the evening listening to a selection from Alain's collection of classical compact discs. By eleven o'clock, when there was still no sign of him, she'd gone to bed, lying awake in the darkness waiting for him return.

She'd had no idea how late it was when she finally succumbed to sleep, springing into wakefulness at the sound of his step outside the door of the main bedroom. In vain she'd waited for his entrance, a terrible loneliness descending on her when she'd realised that she was destined to spend the second night of her married life by herself.

It wasn't that she resented Alain's reticence to become her lover. In truth she had every sympathy with the press-

ures of business which had overshadowed her own
position in his life, but she had hoped he'd feel able to
share his tribulations with her. Nothing would have
pleased her better than to hold him in her arms and
soothe him into a peaceful, restorative sleep. Now she
was beginning to realise, whatever role he had devised
for her, being his confidante and companion was no part
of it!

'Yes?' She turned towards the door as a knock
sounded on its outside.

'Ah, you're up and dressed, good!' Alain came briskly
into the room, casually garbed in fawn leisure trousers
and a dark brown silk knit shirt. Instantly her heart
responded to his presence by increasing its beat in a rush
of expectation. 'I plan to visit Sans Souci after breakfast
to see how the interior decorations are progressing.'

'Sans Souci? How romantic.' Alex smiled delightedly.
'I assume you're referring to the house you're buying?'

'Mmm.' He nodded. 'I take no credit for the name
though, that wasn't my idea.' His voice was clipped as
if refuting any insinuation of romanticism. 'I hope I
didn't disturb you when I came home last night?'

An odd inflexion in his tone warned Alex that the
question might not be as casually concerned as it
appeared. At a loss as to his motives, she gave slight
shrug of her shoulders. 'Not at all. I went to sleep as
soon as my head touched the pillow. I must say it's a
very comfortable bed.'

'I've always found it so,' he confirmed abruptly. 'I
was later than I'd anticipated because of the many well-
wishers who wanted to congratulate me on my unexpected marriage. In the circumstances it seemed more
considerate to spend the night in the second bedroom.'

His dark brows lifted slightly as if he were challenging her to dispute his decision. Some inner caution warned her not to rise to his bait.

'You must do whatever you think best, Alain,' she told him coolly. 'Perhaps as you're eager to get out this morning we should have breakfast straight away? You'll have to tell me what you want.' Having already inspected the refrigerator and store cupboards the previous day and found them adequately stocked by Madame Latache, whose day began at ten-thirty, Alex was confident of satisfying his needs in that respect at least.

'Coffee and toast will suit me admirably.' He stood back, allowing her to precede him from the bedroom. She moved gracefully, her knife-pleated scarlet skirt teamed with a scarlet blazer over a white cotton 'body'. Without undue vanity she knew she looked good, yet Alain hadn't even offered her a perfunctory kiss as a greeting. It was as if a cool wind were chilling the atmosphere between them and she had no idea what could be wrong—unless—unless her fleeting idea of the day before yesterday had some foundation in fact and Alain was labouring under some self-doubts.

If only they'd spent more time together... Love was such a fierce fire, consuming everything in its path; it was so easy to overlook the basic insecurities and fears that formed a part of everyone's character, and Alain wasn't the kind of man who would easily strip his personality bare to a stranger... Stranger! What on earth was she thinking of? She was his wife—not a stranger! But because she loved him she had no intention of adding to the already heavy load of responsibility he bore! She sighed, softly consoling herself with the thought that when they were in the leisured atmosphere of Corsica everything would fall into place.

Impulsively she turned on her heel as they emerged into the wide hallway, lifting her hands to his face, touching his morning-smooth cheeks with gentle fingers, pushing her weight forward on to her toes so she could touch his mouth with her own—a fleeting caress without pressure or invitation.

'I don't think we said "Good morning" to each other,' she said mischievously, and would have left it at that if he hadn't seized her upper arms in a powerful grip.

'How very remiss of me, *ma femme*!' His mouth sought hers, returning her tribute with interest. It was a bitter-sweet kiss, filling her with an aching poignancy because she fancied Alain gave it under protest, as if, now he had finally signed the contract between them, she was no longer of any importance to him.

Off-balanced by the strength of his body against her, she had to raise her hands to steady herself against his chest, experiencing a sweet narcotic in the hard ecstasy of his mouth which lulled the frightened fears of rejection she had begun to feel. There was just the moment—the taste, the touch, the scent of the dominant man in her arms. When his hands slid downwards following the smooth roundness of her hips, she melted against him, making a muffled exclamation of pleasure.

'You want us to become lovers, *ma chère*?' he whispered against her hair, holding her away from him, so she could look up into his eyes and see an amused tolerance in their honeyed depth: an amusement not entirely successful in disguising the suspicion of pain that lurked behind them. 'I find your impatience very flattering, but don't worry, sweet Alex, I have every intention of sharing your bed when the time is right. After all, there's no hurry, is there? We have all our lives in front of us?'

'Is something wrong, Alain?' She met his gaze fearlessly, shocked by the way he'd dismissed her response to his actions.

'Should there be?' He regarded her with serious contemplation. 'To be honest, I thought you looked a little pale this morning, Alex. I hope you haven't picked up some virus?'

Was it her imagination playing tricks on her? The dark, bland face so innocently holding her attention seemed to suggest it might be. Yet she'd never been a victim of her nervous system before! Was it possible that she'd been seeing Alain through rose-coloured glasses and now, away from her own home and the excitement of her wedding-day, the lenses were beginning to shatter? There seemed so little left of the sensitive, vibrant man she'd fallen in love with... Even his professed concern for her health seemed false.

'I'm fine, thank you,' she said a little primly, determined to make the best of the situation. His behaviour might be a little eccentric for a newly married man alone with the wife he loved, but the last thing she wanted to do was give the impression she'd only married him for his body! If he preferred to save the consummation of their love until they were in Corsica, that was fine by her! She thought a little wistfully that she would have been quite satisfied with a kiss and a cuddle in bed, but apparently Alain's idea of togetherness didn't embrace such a simple pleasure!

Sans Souci was even more beautiful than she'd dared to hope. Its two-storeyed white walls with their elegantly proportioned windows were redolent of some of the properties she'd seen featured in *Country Life* but never in her wildest dreams hoped to possess.

As she stepped into the wide hall which doubled as a reception area she could see evidence of the decorators' presence. Paintwork and ceilings positively sparkled with freshly applied paint. Following Alain as he moved through the house, she became increasingly impressed with what she saw. The proportions of every room with its covings, arches and architraves were surely an interior decorator's dream. When the carpets and curtains were in place—and the furniture...

'Did you choose the colour schemes yourself?' she asked him, wondering at this new dimension to his character.

'I'm afraid not.' He flashed her a smile. 'I have a first-rate firm of interior decorators handling everything. I admit I insisted on having the final say, but for the most part it was Claudine they worked with.'

It was so casually said that for a moment the import didn't register with Alex. By the time it did, Alain was already on his way upstairs, climbing the sweeping staircase with purposeful tread.

'Claudine?' She caught him up on the landing, her heartbeat responding to the sudden flood of adrenalin which the name had engendered. 'Do you mean Claudine Dubois—the daughter of the bank's chairman?'

'That's right.' There was nothing in his tone to alarm her as he flung open one of the doors to reveal a spacious bedroom, but already tentacles of fear held Alex in their grasp. Tony's description forcefully echoed in her brain— 'a ravishing teenage daughter called Claudine who was being groomed to become Madame du Gard'.

'How kind of her to let you have the benefit of her expertise,' she returned carefully, trying to make light of what every instinct warned her was a threatening situation.

'Not really,' Alain's voice was calm, almost disinterested, 'since at the time she intended to live here with me as my wife.' His eyes narrowed thoughtfully as he regarded the delicate floral wallpaper. 'On second thoughts I think I was too indulgent when I agreed to this. Something plainer would be more to my taste; what do you think?'

'I agree with you.' Keeping cool with an almighty effort, Alex answered him in the same impersonal tone with which he'd addressed her. 'When exactly did Claudine change her mind—if it's not too personal a question?'

'It's hardly personal since most of Paris already knows.' With the sangfroid which characterised most of his actions, Alain walked across the room to examine the paintwork round the windows. 'Our engagement was about to be officially announced on her twentieth birthday two days ago. However, it seems that in my absence on business in England she met and fell in love with a young Italian who's making his name as one of the new avant-garde fashion designers. The first I knew about it was when Giselle phoned me in Bradford and told me of their elopement. Apparently, because of Luigi Contradini's newsworthiness and Claudine's fortune, the event was splashed on all the front pages of the Paris Sunday scandal-sheets.'

There was no emotion on the countenance of the hard-faced man who was demolishing her dreams with every indifferent word, as her blood chilled. Her nerves screaming, she knew she had to keep her dignity. Her future happiness would depend on it. Drawing in a deep breath, only her tightened fists betraying her agitation as they curled, driving her nails into her palms, she stared at the rigid back view presented to her.

'Two days ago?' Her voice cracked slightly, to be brought immediately under control. 'That was the day we were married.'

'It seemed appropriate.' Alain half turned towards her, lifting a casual shoulder. 'This house was already bought, decorations were under way... and I don't take easily to being made a fool of, so the obvious solution was to replace her intended position in my life without delay.' He turned to face her fully, sweeping her stunned figure with a speculative, approving glance. 'I count myself very fortunate that you were suitable, available and willing at short notice. Believe me, my dear, I don't underestimate the size of the debt I owe you.'

'But you loved her!' Nothing made sense, only the very real pain that seared through her system, tightening her diaphragm, making breathing an effort. Her hand clasping her midriff in an attempt to alleviate the agony which had caught at her, Alex responded instinctively. 'You loved Claudine!'

'A rather sentimental concept, surely?' Dark eyebrows rose, mocking her, while Alain's eyes mesmerised her with their intensity. 'She was an ideal partner for me: connected by business, wealthy in her own right, socially acceptable, well versed in supervising the running of the kind of household I wished to have, young and healthy, capable of giving me heirs and attractive enough to make me the envy of many of my contemporaries.'

'You assessed her as if she were some company you intended to take over?' Alex could hardly believe what she was hearing. He had to be playing some obscene joke on her, only there was nothing in his stance or expression to confirm that hope. She had no idea of the horror mirrored on her face as she questioned him, biting her lip in dismay as he turned impatiently from her.

'You suggest I should have paid less attention to my own personal affairs than I would to a company balance sheet? Isn't that rather naïve, Alex—particularly as your own credit balance was so impressive?'

'I thought...' She couldn't finish the sentence as her whole concept of their relationship exploded like a supernova. She'd thought he'd fallen in love with her in very much the same way as she had with him. Now he was telling her she had been a second-best choice to fulfil an embarrassing gap in his life.

'You thought I'd fallen in love with you?' For the first time he smiled gently as he neatly fielded her thoughts. 'I admit to a lack of self-control after our visit to Epsom. I can only plead an untypical reaction to the irritation of Claudine's thoughtlessness and selfish defection added to the frustration of six weeks away from Paris.'

Did he mean sexual frustration? Alex wondered. Perhaps in Paris he solved any problems in that area by discreet visits to accommodating ladies if Claudine was unavailable! Perhaps now he was back in the capital he'd already renewed those old *friendships*, which would account for his lateness last night and his obvious lack of interest in her own physical charms!

Memories flooded back to her—Alain's change of attitude after his return from Bradford, the way he'd put her through a third degree before inviting her to Epsom. She'd thought she was being interviewed for the position of companion, not wife—yet even then his plans had been made!

It had been a face-saving exercise intended to preserve his reputation and his ego—but why her? Unfortunately the answer was only too obvious. It had been her availability not her irresistibility that had been the deciding factor, and oh, how expertly he'd played his hand arousing a myriad emotions—anger, outrage, curiosity— manipulating her responses to achieve his ends!

'And if I'd allowed myself to be seduced by you that night?' she asked, hardly believing she was still able to carry on a rational conversation. 'I suppose I would have failed the test you set for a prospective wife?'

'But you didn't, did you?' The retort came swiftly, denying her the satisfaction of a straight answer. 'You merely confirmed the impression I'd already formed of you. A beautiful woman, clever enough to use her attributes to their best advantage, and with an eye to the future. What more could I ask for?'

'Mercenary, you mean?' Try as she might, she couldn't keep the quiver from her voice.

'A hard word, *ma chère*.' He appeared amused by her discomposure. 'I would prefer to say "with a good business head"—a quality which appeals to me far more than maudlin sentimentality. I have great respect for a woman who can appear dressed in couturier models a few weeks after the designs have been shown, especially when she is not obviously from the leisured classes.'

'They weren't originals!' Horrified by his assessment of her cupidity, she could only stare at his face which had become that of a stranger.

'Naturally not,' he accorded, 'but quality imitations don't come cheap, and besides, your predilection for the good life was already a byword in the office—holidays in the Caribbean... Italian sports cars...*non*?' His eyebrows lifted quizzically but he didn't wait for her answer. 'A marriage built on mutual need is far more likely to be successful than one based on immature emotional longings, as I'm sure you agree—else why should you agree to my proposal?'

'Yes, of course.' It was the only answer left to her. She wasn't going to demean herself by protesting that the clothes he'd so admired had been the products of her own diligence, that her extravagant claims had been a joke that anyone with a sense of humour would have appreciated and that, fool that she was, she'd lost her heart to him. Pride made her querulous. 'You must forgive me, however, if I'm not entirely clear how our need is *mutual*. I need financial security, as you've already established, but surely you're entirely self-sufficient? You expect me to believe you felt threatened by a few newspaper articles?'

Harshly his words grated into the peaceful atmosphere. 'I don't take kindly to being made a fool of in front of my peers and, unfortunately lacking the biological supremacy of a hydra, I feel it is time I need a wife to bear my legitimate children, to nourish and cherish them to adulthood, someone I can depend on to fulfill her obligations without default.'

'I suppose I should be flattered...' Tears weren't far from her eyes, but Alex had no intention of betraying their presence to the stony-faced man whose attitude challenged the very basis of everything she'd believed in, as he tore her world of illusion apart, shredding it with the clear-cut tones which had brought so many important deals to satisfactory conclusions.

'Flattery is no part of a business contact.' It was as if he'd read her thoughts. 'A mutual exchange of advantages is all that is needed. I needed to replace Claudine in my life—and quickly—and you had all the right qualifications. You give me all the benefits of a faithful wife and I give you your own bank account to indulge your expensive tastes. Love was never part of the deal, as I remember.'

It was for me! she wanted to scream, but the words stuck in her throat. She was damned if she would let him see how badly he'd hurt her or expose herself for the sentimental fool she'd been. Instead she said with a forced lightness, 'I've always thought the thickness of a man's wallet was one of his most vital personal statistics.'

'*Bien*.' He moved towards the door. 'Shall we inspect the rest of the house?'

'There's just one thing.' She followed him from the room as her stunned spirit began to regain some of its lost vitality. 'Did Claudine choose all the furniture and fabrics as well?'

'With my approval, yes. Do you have any objections?' His raised eyebrows dared her to contest the matter.

'I don't know, since I haven't seen them.' Pride was a hard, tight pain in her chest. 'Since it's going to be my home now and not Claudine's I think I have the right to approve them as well, don't you?'

Lines of irritation brought a frown to Alain's face. 'Claudine has excellent taste on the whole, I'm sure you will like her choice.'

'But I don't know that until I've seen it, do I?' Alex was sweetly insistent, as a hopeless anger drove her into contention.

Their eyes met in open antagonism before Alain shrugged indifferently. 'Since it's so important to you, I'll ask the interior decorators to supply you with their plan, together with material swatches. Will that satisfy you?'

'For a start, yes.' She painted a smile on her lips. 'I'll let you know as soon as possible what changes I want to make.'

'Alex . . .' He turned towards her and she thought she saw the mask of annoyance slip to display an unexpected vulnerability. But she was too shaken by what had occurred between them to take advantage of her suspicions. Her one need was to get away from the man she'd married and try to come to terms with what she'd just discovered away from those golden eyes that seemed capable of piercing through her very soul when they wanted to.

'Yes?' Her chin rose proudly as she looked defiantly into his eyes.

'Nothing—just don't take too long in coming to a decision. I should like to move in here as soon as possible on our return from Corsica.'

'Do you anticipate our leaving Paris soon?'

'Why not?' He regarded her thoughtfully. 'Two days at the most should see my present business settled, and my colleagues would think me a neglectful husband if I delayed it any longer.'

'And of course that would never do.' Her retort was sharp because she was stung that the opinion of his colleagues should take precedence over her own feelings.

'*D'accord*,' he agreed smoothly. 'An image of reliability and attention to duty is one of the most positive attributes a banker can have. Besides...' a demon of wickedness seemed to take possession of his personable features as a long dimple grooved his hard-boned cheeks, '...I find your own eagerness to explore one of the most untouched departments of France a powerful stimulant to my plans.' He glanced down at one sinewy wrist where a gold watch reposed. 'And now I suggest we finish our tour here without further delay. We have an appointment at a jeweller's in the Place Vendôme shortly to fill the gap that exists between your knuckle and your wedding-ring.'

'You're going to buy me an engagement ring? Is that necessary?' She knew she sounded ungracious but her thoughts were in such a turmoil she'd responded instinctively.

'It's part of the package,' he told her easily. 'A symbol of good intent on my part.' There was a slight pause while she digested his insinuation before he added softly, 'I'll leave it to you how you reciprocate.'

CHAPTER NINE

How was she meant to reciprocate? Alex looked at Alain's face with a feeling of utter helplessness. This must be tantamount to the kind of nightmares she'd heard actresses confessing to, where they dreamt they were on a stage in a play they didn't recognise and the script of which they'd never read. In a few moments Alain had demolished all her hopes and beliefs and left her with an aching feeling of emptiness. How could she have been so wrong? It wasn't as if she'd ever given her heart lightly or engaged in meretricious flirtations. The moment she'd realised she loved Alain it had been as if the whole tenor of her life had been lifted into another brighter plane; now she knew the name of that place—Fool's Paradise!

An hour later, sitting silently beside him in the efficient but unglamorous Peugeot he used to drive through the bustling Paris streets, she stared at the bow cluster of diamonds and emeralds which graced her finger. She had no idea how much it had cost. She only knew that if it had been given with love she would have preferred to have obtained it from the costume jewellery department of Au Printemps!

Oddly, her own feelings for Alain remained unchanged. If she'd needed confirmation of their sincerity this would be it. Hurt as she was, her love hadn't altered when it had found alteration... in classic fashion it had remained 'an ever-fixed mark'. Not that that was going to make the coming days any easier to bear...

Gazing out at the wide boulevards, she tried desperately to come to terms with what she'd just learned. Alain was still in love with Claudine. No matter that he'd denied any such feelings, it was clear as crystal that he had married her, Alex, on the rebound. He must have been very badly hurt to react in the way he had— shattered, in fact.

She knew him well enough to know that if his association with Claudine had been purely of a business nature he would have had enough *amour-propre* and authority to cope with the minor embarrassment such an event would have caused his social life. He must have wanted to demonstrate very badly indeed that he had other strings to his bow to have gone to the extent of marrying a woman whom he saw as venal, when he must have had so many other opportunities available to him if he'd been prepared to wait.

She would have liked to have refused to accept the ring he'd bought for her, but it would have been a useless protest. Like herself, its presence was merely for show. Despite his low opinions of her character he'd made it clear he had every intention of sharing her bed, impregnating her, giving her the status of mother to his children in due course...

So many things were becoming clearer: his insistence that she would keep her side of the bargain come what may, his untypical bad temper on his return from Bradford, the speed and dexterity with which he'd played on her susceptibilities... To his credit perhaps he hadn't meant to deceive her so utterly? Probably he'd thought she was aware he wasn't in love with her; after all, he'd never said he was, had he?

She'd been an absurd romantic to give credence to such an idea and for that the fault was hers. A woman in years, she'd been a child in emotional development! If only he hadn't been called to Zurich, if they'd had time to discuss things in an atmosphere of calm and quiet...

There were so many 'if's...

Unthinkingly she twisted the glinting jewel on her hand, the only gesture that betrayed her unrest. Supposing they'd become lovers that evening when the phone had interrupted them? There was nothing she dared read into that incident. Anyone knew that a virile man had no difficulty in making love to a reasonably attractive woman when his body was held in the thrall of frustration and desire. His missing Claudine and sickness at heart because of her betrayal, with no other obliging female associate to hand, it wasn't surprising Alain had turned to the woman he intended to make his bride for comfort.

Love as Alex thought of it had nothing at all to do with it. Equally understandable now was his disinclination to share her bed. Back in Paris, with memories of Claudine saturating the atmosphere, it was incredible he could even look at her without flinching!

So what of the future? She was trapped in a loveless marriage, but time was on her side. It would be useless to tell Alain she wasn't avaricious, that all she wanted was his happiness, but in the coming weeks and months, even years, she might be able to win his affection. When he got to know her better he might even like her. From that beginning who knew what might grow? Trust, dependency, comfort—all had their part to play in marriage. With a bit of luck she might even become indispensable!

She knew that many women who liked to consider themselves 'liberated' might condemn her as totally lacking in pride. She preferred to take a longer view. Why let her own bruised self-esteem come between her and what she wanted in life? Despite everything, what she wanted was Alain du Gard, and she was prepared to fight for his affection when there was no one else waiting to take her place.

'Would you like to eat out, Alex?'

She started as his voice penetrated her thoughts. There was no reason why she couldn't prepare a meal for the two of them in the apartment, but the company of other, happy people would be a welcome therapy. Hopefully he wouldn't take it as a sign of her inherent cupidity or domestic incapability!

'What I'd really like to do,' she said honestly, 'is go up to Montmartre and have one of the delicious crêpes in the pancake house in the square—or is that too touristy for you?'

'Not at all,' he agreed promptly. 'We can park at the bottom of the steps if you like and walk up—give you an appetite?'

'Yes, oh, yes!' Delightedly she turned towards him, in that moment forgetting his charm was only skin-deep, amazed that he too shared her need to exert himself physically, to feel the breeze on his face and the sun on his skin.

Half an hour later, flushed and breathless, Alex looked around with real pleasure at the Place du Tertre with its collection of artists and their easels beneath the trees.

'Oh, no—please——' Suddenly aware that one of the artists had positioned himself in front of her and begun sketching, she made a motion to cover her face. 'I'm not interested in buying a portrait.'

'Then *monsieur* will buy it for you!' Doggedly the young man continued sketching, with sure strokes in charcoal on a light grey pad... 'A memento of a wonderful day!'

A hysterical laugh escaped Alex's lips. If he only knew how inapt that comment was!

'Please! I mean it!'

She went to walk purposefully past him, astonished when Alain, instead of giving him equally short shrift as she'd anticipated, said imperturbably, 'Why not? You may as well have it done, if only because when the others see you carrying it you won't be harassed again.'

Outvoted, resignedly Alex stood still, reluctantly admiring the speed and skill of the street artist. In minutes the portrait was completed, the finished picture handed over to her.

Dear lord! Did she really look like that! She was looking at the face of a beautiful woman—far too beautiful to be a true likeness, although she could detect some similarities—but it was a face of almost naked vulnerability. This was no composed career woman in charge of her life: this was a woman whose heart and soul were mirrored in the seemingly empty depths of her eyes. A few strokes of charcoal and he'd exposed her innermost feelings! Alex swallowed miserably as Alain handed over a fistful of francs.

'You shouldn't have done that,' she said quietly as he took possession of the portrait, holding her arm to lead her towards the restaurant. 'It's just a tourist trap, you know.'

'Perhaps.' He didn't seem too disturbed by her allegations. 'On the other hand, it's quite a good likeness. Don't forget Van Gogh and Renoir had to start somewhere. We might have bought our children a masterpiece. Regard it as an investment—I do.'

Alain had been right. She couldn't fault the designs Claudine had chosen for Sans Souci. Poring over the layouts the following morning in the company of Geneviève Lafitte, the director of the company organising the work, Alex had to admit that it was one thing to have ideas about furnishing the normal semi or detached house in suburbia. Sans Souci was different. Built on a far larger scale, it had totally different requirements, and these she had to admit had been met with flair and imagination.

'I think you've done a marvellous job,' she told her companion frankly. 'The only room I have qualms about is the main bedroom.'

'All the frills and furbelows?' Geneviève Lafitte's intelligent eyes twinkled. 'A very romantic setting— almost a boudoir, wouldn't you say?' Both women looked at the flounced bedspread, the garlanded frilled curtains, the layer upon layer of lace around the lampshades, the floral wallpaper and the long-pile white carpet. 'I must admit Monsieur du Gard had his reservations, but the young lady who was with him at the time was most insistent, and in the end he agreed to her having her choice.' She cast Alex a speculative look. 'If you would like to see what Monsieur du Gard himself preferred...?' She paused delicately.

'Please!' Eagerly Alex watched while Geneviève turned to the back of the book, drawing a gasp of pleasure when she saw the same room transformed by a plain grained eau-de-Nil satin paper on the walls, windows concealed by a marvellous printed cotton sateen featuring enormous stylised exotic flowers in a palette selection of pale blues and greens on twining stems, over which the odd bee or butterfly seemed to hover at random.

To her recollection the window had a south-easterly aspect, and she could just imagine the magic of those curtains with the sun behind them. Vibrant and beautiful, they instantly gave her a sense of peace and continuity, and an insight into the complexities of Alain's personality she hadn't suspected. The plain bedcover was a pale coffee, toning in with the short-pile fitted carpet. Not overtly masculine, to Alex the room had a peacefulness and allure which was compelling.

'That's what I want!' She had no hesitation in making a decision, adding a little hesitantly, 'Will it cost a fortune to change it at this late date?'

'Assuredly not.' Geneviève smiled. 'Monsieur du Gard is a very valued customer. We want nothing more than to complete the matter to his satisfaction. Do you have any thoughts about the reading-lamps?'

Inspiration came immediately, Alex's face lighting up with joy. 'Yes, indeed. I'll buy them myself with some of the wedding present money I received from my family.'

Capodimonte, she thought, happily recalling the display she'd seen in the West End of London—beautiful herons delicate and graceful, or perhaps 'Sophie and the Great Dane', the exquisite sculpture of a 1920s slender heroine, proud and beautiful, her china profile lifted proudly, her slim hand resting on the neck of a powerful Great Dane. Evocative and enchanting, the sculptures would look their best beneath plain classic shades which toned with the wallpaper. Instinctively she knew Alain would approve.

Moments later she was showing Geneviève out of the apartment, relieved that her insistence on seeing the designs of her new home had resulted in so very little being changed, and that which had not needing to be confirmed with Alain since his taste was known in advance.

Returning to the sitting-room, she curled up in an armchair, sifting idly through Alain's collection of compact discs, discovering many of her own favourites. After another night spent in separate rooms, this time without any explanation being either necessary or volunteered, Alain had declared his intention of making a final appearance at the *banque* before leaving for

Corsica the following day. After lunch she'd begin to pack. Now she would try to calm her edginess by listening to some music.

Selecting the Weber clarinet concerto, she switched on the CD player, relaxing against the soft cushions surrounding her. The second movement had just started when she heard the front door bell ring and the murmur of voices as Madame Latache gave entry to the unexpected caller.

Help! She hadn't bothered to change out of her casual jeans and cotton top. Suppose it was one of Alain's influential friends...? Jumping to her feet, Alex wondered if she could gain the sanctuary of the bedroom, her effort foiled when Madame Latache opened the door to confront her almost immediately.

'Madame Valais presents her compliments and asks if you are at home today?'

Giselle! Remembering her sister-in-law's warm welcome over the phone, Alex was delighted. 'Yes, of course I am!'

Darting to the door, she threw it wide open, a warm smile of welcome on her face. 'What a lovely surprise! Please do come in.'

Cool and beautiful despite the obvious condition of her pregnancy, Alain's sister stepped across the threshold, her warm smile responding to the spontaneity of Alex's greeting. Wearing a simple dress of navy silk organdie, its large white collar highlighting her pretty face, its accordion-pleated skirt swirling out from just below bust-level, she looked several years younger than the thirty-two Alex knew her to be. She was shorter than Alain by several inches, but the family likeness was unmistakable in the mid-brown eyes and thick, dark hair.

'The weather was so gorgeous I thought I'd take a walk in the Bois,' she explained, pulling her lovely mouth

into a grimace. 'I'm afraid I forgot how all this excess
weight makes one's legs swell!' Ruefully she subsided in
one of the armchairs at Alex's invitation, regarding her
ankles wryly.

'But should you be walking around at all at this stage?'
Alex asked anxiously.

'Pouf!' Giselle's moue of disgust was typically French.
'Children rule one's life after they are born. I shan't be
ruled by this one before he is!' A slim hand resting on
her lap denied the severity of her words as her large eyes
grew apologetic. 'But I did feel a little tired, and as I
was so near...' She hesitated delicately. 'I've no wish to
inconvenience you, but perhaps I could phone for a taxi?'

'Oh, please...' Impulsively Alex touched her arm. 'Do
stay for a while at least. I've been so looking forward
to meeting you. Can I offer you a drink—tea, coffee,
orange...?'

'I do believe you really are pleased to see me!' Giselle
grinned impishly, as her soft eyes scanned Alex's eager
face. 'Orange will be lovely.'

She waited while the other girl slipped outside the room
to ask Madame Latache to supply the refreshments,
continuing as she returned, 'I must admit, I hoped I
might see you today. Both Gerard and Alain will be cross
with me when they find out I called here uninvited, no
doubt.' She shrugged nonchalant shoulders. 'My
husband will be concerned in case I disturbed you and
my brother...' Her expression invited Alex to agree with
her. 'Well, you know Alain. He can be very formal at
times. Partly because he has a very important, responsible job and operates in formal company, but more
particularly I suspect because of the way Papa brought
him up. I'm sure he'd prefer for us to be formally introduced first!' Her eyes sparkled mischievously. 'I'm
hoping you're going to change all that! You can't im-

agine how overjoyed I was to discover that after all these years Alain had fallen head-over-heels in love at last! I'm convinced it's going to be the making of my lovely, impossible brother!'

Alex swallowed miserably, unable to keep up the masquerade. 'You're very kind,' she returned quietly, 'but there's no need to pretend. I know all about Claudine. Alain told me everything.' But not before it was too late, her wounded heart cried out silently.

'Claudine?' Astonishment was mirrored on the French girl's face. 'Well, yes, I suppose he would have had to mention what had happened since she created a front-page scandal, if only to protect you from the gossip of people who didn't know the truth.'

'Truth?' Alex frowned. 'He was in love with her. He was going to marry her. Is there any other truth?'

'Surely he hasn't let you believe that!' Giselle looked horrified. 'For a man who is so perspicacious about most things, in affairs of the heart he is abnormally blind! Of course he didn't love Claudine. She's very young and spoiled, a wilful child who can be quite charming but with no substance. I'm sure he was fond of her in a rather patronising kind of way, but she would have driven Alain mad within two weeks of becoming his wife, as I told him on more than one occasion!'

'But he didn't listen to you,' Alex reminded her gently, wishing with all her heart she could believe what the other girl was telling her so vehemently.

'He was stubborn,' Giselle admitted. 'I think he'd got the desire to settle down and, since he'd never been in love and Claudine's father thought he'd make an ideal son-in-law, and Claudine herself wasn't averse to the idea at the time, he settled for what was available. Mind you,' she added graciously, 'the girl was pretty enough, well-connected enough——'

'And never saddled by another owner!' Alex interrupted cynically without thinking, blushing when she saw Giselle's momentary puzzlement.

'Ah! I see what you mean!' Amusement brought dimples to the corners of her mouth. 'Of course you're right. I'd bet my life they were never lovers. My brother would have far too much respect for her youth and the esteem in which her father held him to compromise her even if he'd been in love with her, which he wasn't! Mind you,' she looked thoughtful, 'I wouldn't stake anything on Luigi Contradini having observed the same proprieties. Our Claudine might be young but she didn't give the impression of being entirely untouched!'

She paused as Madame Latache entered the room bearing a tray of iced orange juice and an assortment of biscuits. Taking a glass and drinking from it with obvious pleasure, Giselle sighed as the housekeeper retreated from the room.

'I don't know what you must think of me, prattling on like this. Generally I'm more circumspect.' She leaned forward confidentially. 'It's the fault of the hormones, you know. When I'm having a baby I feel on top of the world and I'm afraid I become garrulous. But in any case I couldn't have let you go on believing that there was anything of an emotional nature between Claudine and Alain.'

'You're very kind, and I really do appreciate it.' Alex sipped her own drink. She'd just been told what Alain had already told her, and to do her justice her visitor appeared to believe what she was imparting. If Giselle knew just how barren her marriage was she would doubtless change her mind, but as much as she liked her sister-in-law there were some things which couldn't be confided.

'Kindness has nothing whatsoever to do with it,' Giselle defended herself stoutly. 'Believe me, I couldn't have been more delighted when Alain broke the habits of a lifetime to act impulsively and make you his bride within a few weeks of knowing you. I knew then he'd fallen in love at last.' Her eyes swept over Alex's sensitive face, reading the doubt that lingered there. 'I was so afraid his potential for finding real happiness had been stunted by my father's attitude towards women...' She paused as if gathering her thoughts. 'I take it Alain told you that our mother left Papa when we were children?'

'I knew they were divorced, yes,' Alex confirmed. 'He told me too that he hadn't seen your father for fifteen years. He *was* invited to our wedding, you know, but he pleaded ill health via his housekeeper...'

'I know.' Giselle interlaced her fingers in her lap, leaning forward earnestly to pinion Alex's attention. 'It's a very difficult situation, I'm afraid. When Maman left, Papa devoted himself to Alain. He was the only son, the heir to the vineyard Papa owns near Avignon, the hope for the future. The estate has been in the hands of the du Gards for many years, you see. In fact our very name "du Gard" is derived from the surrounding district. But instead of indulging my brother as one might have expected, at times Papa was quite brutal with him—physically and mentally, I'm afraid.'

She looked at Alex with sadness darkening her face. 'Even as a child, I realised what was happening was wrong. My father gave him everything materially, but never overt love or affection. Alain was brought up to hide his emotions, never to show pain or anger and particularly not love! Now I think it was because Papa never wanted him to be so utterly vulnerable as he had been. He never wanted him to be destroyed by a woman.'

'And you, what about you?' Alex asked, shocked by the revelations her sister-in-law was pouring out.

'I was luckier. Whereas Papa took responsibility for Alain personally, I had a nursemaid cum governess who was a lovely lady. I was never put under the terrible pressures my brother suffered.' She looked at Alex, her pretty face serious. 'I hope I'm not doing the wrong thing in telling you all this. In due course, I'm sure Alain will confide in you, only at the moment you seem—you seem a little uncertain about his feelings and I just want you to know that if he has difficulty in showing the soft side of his nature it's not because it doesn't exist. Oh, my dear——!' She broke off in consternation. 'Now I've made you cry!'

'I'm sorry...' Alex dabbed at her eyes with a hastily procured tissue, her heart overflowing with compassion for the man she'd married, deprived firstly of a mother and then of a potential fiancée. At least, she determined furiously, he might not love *her*, but she would never let him down like the two other women in his life, however difficult the years ahead might prove! 'Please do go on—the more I know about his past, the easier it's going to be for me.'

'That's what I thought.' Giselle nodded wisely. 'Well, Papa wanted Alain to go into the wine business, but my brother had other ideas. He was nineteen when he left for Paris to study for a career in banking. I think he would have gone earlier but he needed money to support himself. *Mon Dieu*, Alex, the way that boy worked! Taking on all kind of jobs, from labouring to waiting at table to gain his independence. Not only did he have an aptitude for figures but he was very determined— single-minded, in fact.'

'Yes, I know the details of his career,' Alex assured her, although naturally the details she'd found out included nothing of his earlier trials. Stupidly she'd assumed he'd been put through university by his parents! 'How did your father react to his success?'

Sadly Giselle shook her head. 'I'm afraid by then he'd washed his hands of him entirely. They were like two male lions challenging each other for supremacy. In fact Papa had ordered Alain never to set foot in the family house again. But the truth is…' she smiled sadly '…Papa was inordinately proud of his success—you could see the glow of satisfaction on his face—but he'd never publicly admit it. The tragedy is that he cared, still does care very deeply for Alain.'

'And Alain hates your father?' Secure in the love of her own parents, Alex found it very difficult to restrain the ready tears that still threatened her.

Slowly Giselle shook her head. 'Despite everything it's my belief that my brother both loves and respects him but is too proud to make a gesture of reconciliation because he won't face up to the possibility of another rejection. As a matter of fact I have a plan to get them together, but I'll need your help?'

It was more a question than a statement, and Alex nodded. 'I can't do anything against Alain's will, but I'm prepared to plead your case if you think it'll do any good, although please don't expect too much.'

Giselle smiled radiantly. 'Bless you, Alex! I'll let you into a secret, then. I've managed to persuade Papa that, whatever his feelings for Alain, it would be extremely discourteous and unfitting for a gentleman of his status not to welcome you into the family. I also mentioned that if he wants heirs, then it is *your* children who will bear the name of du Gard.

'It took a bit of doing, I admit, but eventually he agreed to come up to Paris and meet you in my house at a small party I intend to throw to welcome you and

Alain home after your honeymoon. What I need *you* to do is prepare Alain for the encounter and make sure he escorts you.'

'I'm not sure I'll be able to...' With the best will in the world Alex couldn't imagine herself persuading her truculent husband into following any mode of procedure he didn't wish to, and the portents weren't very bright in the circumstances.

'You underestimate yourself, *ma belle soeur*. If I weren't so sure of your success I wouldn't have asked you, but your love for my brother is so obvious, I know he'll melt like the snows in the valley when the sun strikes them. And to tell the truth I've set my heart on having my whole family around me when *numéro trois* is christened.' She smiled with easy charm. 'If anyone can heal the breach between them—it will be you, Alex. Trust me, I know.'

'I'd love to believe that's true.' Alex regarded her wistfully, then added impulsively, 'You don't have to rush away, do you? I was planning to have a light lunch of lobster and salad here in the apartment. Could you stay and share it with me?'

'I'd be delighted to.' There was no gainsaying the pleasure on Giselle's face. 'I'll just have to phone home and leave a message for Gerard or he'll panic if he phones from the office and finds I've disappeared without trace!'

At least Giselle's marriage was a happy one, Alex thought enviously as her guest made the necessary call, and she herself went to acquaint Madame Latache of the new luncheon arrangements, her gratitude for the warmth of the other woman's greeting lending her body a warm glow of pleasure. Alain had forecast that she would like his sister. In fact it was more than that. She felt an empathy with her sister-in-law that was remarkable. It was one of the things that was going to make the coming years a little easier for her to bear.

Over lunch Giselle continued to bring Alex up to date with the family history, describing her early years near Avignon and the strength of her relationship with her brother despite the lack of encouragement it received from their father. Her face lost something of its animation as she spoke of her mother.

'Of course, I don't remember her. I was only three when Papa divorced her. When I was older I persuaded some of the villagers to tell me about her. It seems she was very pretty, half-Italian and full of the *joie de vivre*. Papa was quieter, more reserved and totally committed to his business. It was the old story. It seems she wanted more attention than he was prepared or able to give her...' Her shoulders lifted disparagingly. 'The summer their marriage finally fell apart, Papa took on some extra hands for the vintage and among them was this young Italian. The story goes that Papa found them together and ordered her out of the house.

'Whether she pleaded for forgiveness or not I don't know... I don't even know if she wanted to take us with her...everyone said she was a loving and caring mother... In any case Papa would never have agreed—so—that's it, I'm afraid. As far as I know he never looked at another woman after she left. My own feeling is that he loved her very much but lacked the ability to give her the emotional support she needed, and when he found she'd been unfaithful it just broke his heart, which is why I make allowances for the way he behaved.'

She met Alex's concerned gaze with something bordering on fervour illuminating her countenance. 'It's only these last few months that I've detected a softening in his attitude. For a man like Papa to lose both his wife and his son must be an intolerable burden. Nothing can be done about the first—but Alain...' She paused before adding with quiet purpose, 'Alain is strengthened now by finding his own fulfillment in life and love and I feel positive that between us you and I can make our stubborn menfolk heal a breach that has been left gaping for far too long!'

'I wish I shared your certainty about my own abilities of persuasion,' Alex said softly, unable to hide her own self-doubt from the intelligent eyes of her companion.

'*Courage, ma chère*! Your only problem is that Alain played the buccaneer rather than the courtier and spirited you away before you had time to break down the defensive wall he builds round himself.' She paused tellingly. 'Believe me, Alex, my dear, my brother may not weep or show evidence of pain inflicted on him, but cut him—and he bleeds as much as you or I!'

It was late afternoon before Giselle departed by taxi, leaving Alex in a much happier frame of mind than previously. Not that she'd changed her opinion about Alain's feelings for Claudine, or that the hurt occasioned by his reference to the matter had in any way lessened. No, she determined, the rise in her spirits was because she now felt reasonably assured that Alain would want to make a success of their marriage however specious its basis.

Time would make his pain at Claudine's loss more bearable, and, if he was as vulnerable as Giselle suspected, when in the future he needed comfort—either emotional or physical—then she, Alex, would be there to provide it. It wasn't what she'd wanted, but because she loved him it was what she'd settle for. The alternative was unthinkable.

CHAPTER TEN

ALAIN came striding up the beach towards her. Watching him, Alex realised how his clothes had tended to underplay the rugged masculinity of his build, their fluid line disguising the firmly developed muscles of his upper legs and calves, the smooth power lying dormant in his broad shoulders, the full beauty of that wickedly graceful male body.

She'd been watching him as he windsurfed, feasting her eyes on him as, body arched, arms taut against the strain of the sail, the sun burnishing his golden body, he'd cut through the water with the spray glistening on his thighs and the silence of the open sea engulfing him.

Now he came across the deserted arc of sand, stopping within metres of her, smiling down at her, his eyes narrowed against the reflected glare of the sun, the tanned expanse of skin on show shimmering with the patina of sea-salt. He could have been a pirate, a beach-comber, even a movie star—anything but a merchant banker, she considered lazily as her eyes drifted admiringly over him, marvelling at the quality of the tan he'd managed to acquire in just two days' exposure to the sun. But then of course his pigmentation was naturally darker than her own; after all, his mother had been half-Italian...

'Are you just looking—or are you interested in buying?' The question spoken in a soft drawl took her by surprise, as did the upward slant of his mouth and the gleam of meaning in the topaz eyes that demanded her attention.

157

Alex felt the breath catch in her throat, her whole body tensing beneath the floral halter-necked backless swimsuit in which she'd chosen to sunbathe. They'd been in Corsica for two days and two nights: a man and woman sharing the same beautiful villa, occupying separate bedrooms, eating and relaxing together, enjoying civilised, non-controversial conversations, carefully avoiding any real issues between them.

Neither of them had mentioned Claudine. Sick at heart though she was, Alex had made a tremendous effort to act as normally as possible, sensing there was no profit in it for her to attempt to force an unwelcome intimacy on Alain. Her only hope, she'd determined, was to be her usual self and hope and pray that eventually her husband might find himself growing to like her! Love was something different again although, she'd comforted herself, many examples of love growing from mutual liking and respect existed. It was the most she could ever hope for.

'Isn't that what the lady usually asks the gentleman?' she asked with assumed light-heartedness through lips suddenly dry beneath their protective sunscreen, half glad, half terrified at the message she could detect on his intense countenance.

'I've always been interested in buying.' He dropped down beside her in one smooth action of co-ordinated muscle and sinew. 'You're far too perspicacious ever to have doubted that, my lovely Alex.'

Having him so close to her, naked except for the brief bathing-shorts that concealed but in no way detracted from his masculinity, was doing dreadful things to her nervous system. She heard the challenge in his cryptic admittance, but had no time to analyse it as he leaned over her, placing his damp hands with infinite care on her flushed cheeks, pushing her back on her inflated sunbed so that she sprawled full length beneath the shade of the sun umbrella.

Gasping with shock and delight as he brought his own body down upon her, tasting her mouth with cool, salty lips, she found the dampness of his flesh shockingly erotic as it touched her burning skin where it lay open to the kiss of the sun.

Drops of sea-water trickled from his body, running down the cleft between her firm, thrusting breasts as he slid one hand sinuously over the flat planes of her abdomen.

'You win, my darling.' His voice was hoarse. 'I want you now, Alex, soft and naked beneath me, giving me everything you can, not holding back. You won't regret it. Whatever your reasons for marrying me you can pretend, can't you? Make it good for both of us and I'll see you'll never regret what you've done...'

His weight compressed her, emphasising the urgency of his plea. Frightened by the anguish on his face, she tried to escape the pressure of his body, panic rising in her throat as she read his deep dislike for what he believed her to be. He was virtually asking her to earn her keep, to pay with her body for the dresses and jewellery, the apartments and care for which he still imagined she'd agreed to become his wife.

Her breath escaped in a sob, at the irony of his asking her to pretend what was only too real. If only it would be as simple as that! But it also seemed he was asking for a level of expertise she was far from possessing. Not that she was lacking in theoretical knowledge—only its practical application. In a normal loving relationship, instinct would have sufficed, but with Alain about to close his eyes and imagine she was Claudine she doubted if her instinct, burdened by the knowledge that she was merely the instrument to assuage his frustration, would be capable of satisfying a man of his maturity, experience and obvious virility.

'What is it, *chérie*?' Brilliant eyes, their pupils distended and mesmeric, pinioned her own gaze from a distance of centimetres.

She couldn't find the words she needed to defuse the situation, staring helplessly at him, noticing the fine lines at the outer corner of his eyes, the gleam of salt which matted his dark lashes.

Somehow, despite the demon which was riding him, he was sensitive to her fear even if he didn't understand its source. 'I won't hurt you, Alex! By everything that's holy, whatever you've done, for whatever reason you married me, I swear I won't hurt you...' He pushed a lock of hair away from her forehead with fingers that trembled with pent-up tension. 'I won't hurt you in any way at all, ever... Come back to the villa with me—now!' His hands gripped her wrists.

She should be grateful for his assurance of gentleness—and she was! But it was no substitute for a word of affection. Bitterness welled within her. She was supposed to pretend to love him, but he had no intention of returning the compliment! He was asking her for sex as if he'd met her on the street... Unfortunately because she loved him she had no alternative but to accept his terms.

'If that's what you want,' she agreed, her voice shaking, instantly aware of his sigh of triumph mingled with relief. 'I just hope I won't disappoint you.'

'You won't!' He sprang to his feet, pulling her upright, his tone thick with the hunger that surged through him, priming his vital male body for action. 'I won't let you!'

A lick of fear feathered Alex's spine at the implication in his last words, equally matched with a deeper, more insistent sensation as if a coil were being tightly wound inside her preparing her for unknown dangers and delights.

Taking her hand, Alain started to walk swiftly along the beach towards the sandy track which led to the villa, pulling her with him, breaking into a run when they were a few metres distant from their destination.

Confused by the myriad feelings and emotions which streamed through her mind and body, she stumbled, half falling. Sweeping her up into his arms as easily as if she'd been a child, Alain laughed like a carefree adolescent at her startled face, burying his face in her wind-blown hair as he covered the remaining distance.

Life and exuberance flowed through him, turning him into a god—a latter-day Hercules—burning and swift and divine, sturdy of limb and sure of purpose, Alex thought wildly, as, cradling her to his heart, he mounted the short flight of stairs.

Brilliant sunshine streamed through the wooden slats of the dark green shutters, turning the white bedroom into a zebra quilt as he deposited her against the coolness, standing over her, broad chest heaving with effort, hands splayed on hips across which the patterned cotton of his bathing-trunks formed an inconsequential splash of colour.

'Alain...' Alex whispered his name, tasting its syllables, flirting with it, too conscious of the brute strength of his hard male body to be entirely at ease. For her own sake she ought to try and tell him that she'd never had a lover, but somehow the words he might believe refused to form in her mind.

'Yes, *ma petite*?' His reply was slurred with anticipation, his eyes only for her panting body as he lowered himself to the bed, reaching for and withdrawing the halter neck of her swim-suit, so that the garment pooled in a heap of bright colour beneath her navel.

A warm prickling sensation intensified on her forearms, as if a charge of electricity had been fed through her, as he bent his head to tease the dusky pink tip of one still-pale breast, and as it grew marble-hard between his attentive lips she heard his sigh of pleasure.

Every cell of her skin where it touched his was flashing a message of delight back to her befuddled mind, her whole body responding to him, awakening to the delicacy and sureness of his gentle mouth and the long, predatory fingers that were enslaving her into a mindless pleasure. Desire was a warm stream running through her veins, making her soft and pliant beneath him, but with it was a thread of lingering fear, tempering her response.

'Please,' she murmured, her mouth answering his ardour by tasting the salty satin texture of his facial skin, 'be gentle with me...'

It was a plea born of ignorance, and it was only when Alain gazed down at her, the warm darkness of his eyes devouring her with lust, that she realised he thought she was talking from experience.

'Tell me what you like.' The words were wrung from his lips with great effort as his fingers moved with lazy eloquence over her glowing flesh, dragging the swimsuit from her body, replacing its scant cover with his own mind-shattering caresses. 'Is this what you want, my darling? Is this how your lovers pleasured you?' He was tantalising her with exquisite patience and control until the fear she'd felt at the first touch of his intimately exploring hand was replaced by the fear he would withdraw it too soon!

But his words were horrific! Gone was the tender, passionate drawl of the lover, to be replaced by the harsh tones of a man who thought himself only tolerated for what he could provide.

He would possess her because his physical need outweighed any other consideration, but mentally and emotionally he still rejected her. She was still a golddigger, a woman who had married a rich man without compunction, and that was how, in the end, he was going to take her, not only without love, but without compassion, castigating her, not only for her own supposed sins, but for those of the other unfaithful women in his life—his mother and Claudine! It was more than she could bear.

'No...' she moaned, twisting her body beneath his weight in a blind panic, writhing helplessly beneath his confining bulk. 'Not like this...'

'What's wrong with this? Tell me, Alex. Tell me what you want; you'll find I'm a good learner if the rewards are good enough.' He kissed her deeply with a savage passion that stunned her into silence.

'*Viens, mon ange.*' His tone was langourous now, but with an underlying current of excitement that showed how thin his line of self-control had been stretched. 'I've waited all this time to enjoy you; don't go cold on me now!' Without warning his voice roughened. 'For heaven's sake, Alex—don't make me take you; can't you give me anything—anything at all?'

Not like this, she couldn't. Not spread-eagled, held responsible for nameless crimes not of her own doing, struggling against his demanding body, her breath sawing painfully with effort, feeling and resenting the tense line of violence which was an integral part of his desire for her.

'You don't understand,' she sobbed at last in desperation.

'Oh, but I do.' His sweet hands were as gentle as his voice now. 'Much more than you think! But we've always wanted each other, from the very first day our eyes, not to mention our personalities, clashed across a desk! Forget him, Alex! He was never worthy of you!'

Forget who? Confused, she made one last violent effort to escape his purposeful male body, but he was beyond the reach of her distress, lost in his own world of sensual pleasure as his hands and mouth brought her skilfully to a state of submission that had nothing to do with the icy coldness of her mind or sickness of her spirit.

Yet, when he murmured soft, erotic words of love to her in French, tender, subtle compliments, she was moved by their magic as well as the evidence of his own over-powering need for her.

'Alain, *mon amour, mon bien-aimé . . .*' She slid her hands down the lean, muscled length of his superb body, now naked beneath her exploring fingers, her sobs turning to gasps of pleasure as his hands went on the sheet each side of her and she felt the full, sweet strength of his vigorous male body against her own—vital and virile . . .

It was then she screamed. A high-pitched, gasping sound from the back of her throat, piercing the stillness of the sun-baked afternoon. Not because of the pain, for there was little, but because he had possessed her at last and she in her turn had taken him, cradling him in the soft velvet heat of her being, using her fine young body in a celebration of desire fulfilled, rising and falling to the rhythm he initiated, taking an almost unbearable pleasure in knowing he was completely without control, dependent on her for his ultimate release. His face was strangely pale, the tawny eyes shuttered and empty as she nurtured and encouraged him to the final release, her triumph complete when he shuddered to a powerful climax before collapsing against her, his head buried against her shoulder.

There had been no earth-shaking culmination for her, but every muscle of her body pulsated with vibrant life. Alain hadn't been disappointed and that was her satisfaction. It was something to build on for the future. Her hand rose tenderly to caress the crisp dark hair, unruly and tangled on his forehead. Closing her eyes, she smiled.

She must have drifted into sleep, exhausted by physical effort and the enervating effect of a morning in the sun, because when she next became aware of the room and its contents Alain was nowhere to be seen, but before leaving her he'd covered her lower body with the cotton sheet.

Sighing, she swung her legs out of bed. Probably he'd gone downstairs and helped himself to the sea-food salad that was already prepared in the fridge for their lunch. For herself, she had no appetite. Neither did she feel able to face her husband yet. She needed more time to become adjusted to the fact that their marriage had finally been consummated and to ponder on what the outcome of that consummation might be.

Making her way to the en-suite bathroom, she entered, standing beneath the shower, enjoying the cascading water as she lathered herself with shower gel. Cool and refreshed, she stepped out, wrapping herself in a large towel, going through the motions of drying herself, hoping that Alain wouldn't come looking for her—and nearly positive that he wouldn't.

What she needed now was time to herself, and she had a very good idea of where she might find it. Behind the villa on a high ridge she'd noticed the ruins of an old Genoese tower. Using that as a landmark, she'd walk through the sweet-smelling *maquis*, alone with her thoughts.

Quickly she pulled on a stretch Lycra top, sleeveless and low-necked, its fuchsia-pink bright against the brief-

cuffed champagne-coloured shorts she chose to pair with
it, and slipped her feet into espadrilles. A quick spray
of high-factor, non-oily sun protection over her exposed
skin and she was ready to escape from the oppressive
atmosphere in the silent villa. She would exit by the back
door, hopeful that Alain would be eating in the dining-
room and she'd pass by unobserved. When next she saw
him she would have gathered her thoughts and planned
her next course of action.

The encounter would be much easier for her than if
she came upon him now while her heart ached as much
for the want of his love as her body did from the effects
of its bestowal.

Breathing a sigh of relief, she reached the door
undetected and let herself out into the shimmering heat
of the early afternoon. She located the tower on the
horizon and, turning towards it, she started walking,
honeyed air bathing her in its perfume, the only
disturbing sound the incessant chorus of cicadas.

After a while the track she'd chosen petered out, but
she was able to pick her way carefully through the prickly
undergrowth, fixing her eyes on the goal she'd set for
herself. It was hard going, and stout walking shoes would
have been a better choice than espadrilles, she registered
a trifle ruefully, but the physical effort was proving a
splendid catharsis, rescuing her from self-pity.

Alain might not love her, but he'd truly worshipped
her with his body, although the register office ceremony
had contained no such exhortation, and despite her
reservations she'd responded to him as genuinely as she
had instinctively that first night near Epsom, and at the
last moment with her hands gripping the driving beauty
of his thrusting body she'd welcomed him to herself with
abundant love. Was it purely wishful thinking to suppose

that somewhere deep within himself Alain might have recognised the depth of her feelings for him after all?

'Whatever your reasons for marrying me,' he'd said. Cruel words that even now, hours later, brought a sharp pain to her chest—or was it the unusual exertion of the climb after all that emotional trauma? Reaching the shade of the tower at last, she sat in its darkness. The truth was Alain desired her and she both desired and loved him. They'd been married a handful of days. Days bedevilled with misunderstanding and disillusionment—and now this. It had to be a new beginning. Somehow she would ensure that it was.

Sitting in solitary silence, she stared out towards the sparkling sea, watching the sun sink lower in the heat-bleached sky, totally unaware of the passage of time, feeling the hurt and bitterness slowly draining from her. Too soon to tell Alain she loved him, because that would expose her naked soul to his cynicism, but she would try her damnedest to wean his love away from Claudine in any way open to her in an attempt to make her marriage, if not the scented bed of roses she'd dreamed about, at least a workable partnership.

Dusk was beginning to fall when she started on the long walk downwards. It should have taken a fraction of the time spent in climbing, but after struggling on for about an hour she realised with a growing sense of horror that the last rays of the sun were sliding from sight beneath the horizon and that she was utterly lost.

Surrounded by thick scrub, she felt as if she were drowning in a sweet-smelling, vicious sea of thorns, with no place to sit or rest. Fighting down her rising panic, she did the only thing possible—continued walking, forcing her way through the cruel barriers, waist and shoulder high at times, heedless of the thorns that ripped her bare legs and pricked against her upper body, tearing at her flimsy top and lacerating her naked arms, praying that in time she must reach some kind of track or road, refusing to consider the alternative because the implications were too grim!

She hadn't thought to cry for help in that wilderness until she saw the light. As she breasted through a particularly thick wedge of bushes her pulse quickened with relief as she saw a white glow ahead of her moving slowly in a semi-circle. It was probably a shepherd, but even a bandit would be a welcome sight, she thought hysterically, admitting for the first time how close to the limit of her courage she had come.

'*Au secours*!' she cried out. 'Help me, please help me!'

The light stopped swinging as her clear, terrified voice carried cleanly through the warm night air. Then the miracle happened. Alain's voice floated back to her, sharp with anxiety. 'Alex! For goodness' sake, where are you?'

'Here!' she screamed, knowing 'here' was nowhere, but having no means of identifying her whereabouts.

'OK. Stay where you are, I'll find you. Watch the torch and guide me towards you.' He spoke calmly, dissolving her fear as the light began to move slowly but inexorably in her direction.

'Oh, Alain . . .' She was close to tears when he reached her, hair tousled and matted, clothes filthy from the bark of the shrubs, every visible portion of her skin marked by thorns, her legs caked with dried blood, her breath coming in heavy gasps. 'Oh, Alain, I thought I was lost.' She clung to him as he lifted her easily into his arms, taking solace in his strength.

'Yes.' His tone was grim, loaded with anger, his face harshly drawn, the hands that held her lacking in gentleness. 'So did I. We'll talk about it when I get you home.'

Home, she thought. What a beautiful word. It was wonderful to be held secure in his powerful arms, to feel the thud of his steady heart against her own breast. Burying her face against his neck, she savoured the sweet spiciness of his warm skin, preparing herself to suffer his wrath for her irresponsibility, heart-sick because it wasn't the way she'd hoped to start their future relationship.

In her blind descent she must have come unknowingly closer to the villa than she could have dared to hope, because Alain carried her all the way back, even up the stairs to the bedroom as he'd done hours earlier, laying her gently down on the bed. Now there was only compassion and concern in his amber eyes as she whispered her thanks.

Subdued and still unnerved by her escapade, she watched silently as he returned from the bathroom with a bowl of warm water and some cotton wool. Carefully he seated himself beside her, beginning to bathe the long, curving gashes on her bare legs.

'I'm afraid some of these cuts are going to leave scars for several weeks,' he told her grimly, his dark head bent over his task. '*Mon Dieu*, Alex!' Anger flared suddenly, deepening his tone. 'Do you know what a dangerous thing you did? People have got lost in the *maquis* and died before help could reach them!'

She bit her lip, chastened by his fury. 'It was stupid of me. I'm afraid I just didn't think. I'm sorry.'

'Sorry!' He laughed bitterly without humour. 'I don't blame you for wanting to run away from me after what happened. I deserve nothing better—but to have your death on my conscience...' He shuddered, not meeting her astonished gaze.

'You think I was running away—but why?'

For a long moment it seemed she was to receive no answer, and she stared at his capable, gentle fingers as they ministered to her wounds. Then with a deep sigh he laid the towel down, turning his clear gaze to meet her puzzled look.

'Are you telling me you're prepared to stay with me after what I've done to you? The way I betrayed what you felt for me originally, the brutality I subjected you to earlier today?'

She must be delirious, poisoned by the thorns, because what he said didn't make any kind of sense. Alex heaved in a deep breath, fighting to clear her mind. If she wasn't careful she would betray the profundity of her feelings, embarrassing him with her unwanted emotion. Swallowing the sudden lump in her throat, she made a deliberate effort to keep her voice light.

'I think I'd look rather stupid if I packed my bags and went back to England so soon, don't you?' she asked, hoping that by responding to his question with another one she would steer a safe path through what appeared to be an emotional minefield. 'Besides,' she added as the thought struck her, 'what would Giselle think?' She'd already told him of his sister's welcome visit, but naturally nothing of their conversation concerning himself!

'The truth, possibly.' His dark face was grim beyond description. 'That I'd driven you away by an incredible performance of insanity, arrogance and bestiality!'

'Alain!' Shocked, she pushed herself into a sitting position. 'You're no brute! Arrogant, I grant you, headstrong and wilful perhaps, but never, never a brute!' Her fingers sought the springy dark hair that graced his scalp, aware that his whole body tensed at her touch.

'Did you bring any antiseptic ointment with you?' To her utter disappointment he recoiled from her, a rough edge to his voice which had nothing to do with impatience as he rose to his feet.

'Yes, on the bathroom ledge.' She watched him walk through the doorway, too sensitive not to perceive that the relationship between them was changing shape or to experience hope mixed with dread at the metamorphosis taking place.

More knowledgeable than she about the danger of the *maquis*, he'd dressed with considerably more intelligence, she observed. His thick black denim jeans and long-sleeved cotton shirt in the same colour would certainly have protected his skin against the worst of the barbs, but she hadn't been the only one injured. She'd seen the scratches on Alain's hands, and there was one deep one on his left cheek where the blood had dried in a hard slash of colour, suggesting that speed rather than caution had been the driving force behind his search for her.

Returning with the cream, he started to apply it to the inflamed marks on her legs, concern in every taut line of his face. She'd felt his fear for her welfare in the warmth of his arms as he'd carried her, was increasingly conscious of it now as he smoothed the cream into the cleaned cuts with caring fingers. It might not be the same kind of love as she felt for him, but it was better than nothing.

'There!' He finished his ministrations, putting down the empty tube. 'I think you'll survive after some supper and a good night's sleep.' He hesitated. 'Tomorrow, when you feel better, we have to talk.'

Tomorrow be damned! Every instinct told Alex that if she was to resurrect anything worthwhile from this drama it would be now, tonight!

'I'm sorry, Alain . . .' she contrived to look contrite as inspiration came to her aid '. . . but I think I've got some scratches on my back as well—can you help me off with my top?' Her voice was shaky as he shot her a quick, speculative look, but she managed to keep the innocence of her expression unchanged.

'Of course.' He lifted the garment easily away from her. 'You're right, there are a few, but fortunately they're not deep.'

'There was another one!' She'd detected the sudden huskiness in his voice, but he'd made no attempt to keep contact with her body. Quickly she unhooked her bra, cupping her breast and seeking to examine its underside. 'Yes, look! A deep thorn-mark!'

She wasn't lying. A dark, pitted puncture already showing bruising around its circumference marred her soft skin.

'I'm sorry, there's no cream left.' Alain spoke harshly, moving as if to leave her, as desperately she raised a hand to detain him. What had she to lose anyway?

'When I was small my mother used to kiss me better,' she babbled. 'It always worked!' Wide, beseeching eyes searched his troubled face, inviting his response.

'No!' he bit out harshly. 'I beg you, Alex—don't punish me like this!'

'It's not a punishment,' she protested, encouraged by the vehemence of his response, knowing with a sense of triumph that he wasn't unmoved. Deliberately she reached towards him as he still hesitated, forsaking her last shred of pride, drawing his head down, her soft lips caressing the scratch on his cheek with soft, pecking kisses, drifting downwards to caress its fiery tail with her tongue.

Beneath her mouth, his skin was alive and warm, his pulses hammering, his blood beginning to sing with arousal. Talk indeed! The language of love was a powerful tongue. She might not be fluent in it—and, heaven knew, her first lessons had been traumatic—but she was a linguist, wasn't she? If she had a good enough teacher, she'd learn.

'That feels better, doesn't it?' She smiled provocatively at him, watching his pupils darken and cloud with a powerful awareness.

'What do you want, Alex?' he asked hoarsely.

'Well, nothing unless it's willingly given.' Her voice shook. It wasn't as easy as she'd hoped. She could try to seduce him, but she couldn't beg for his love. Tears of shame blurred her eyes as she reached blindly for her discarded top, humiliated by her failure.

'Alex... my darling love...' Strong arms wrapped around her. 'For heaven's sake, don't weep! Don't you understand I can't accept this from you, if I want to retain the smallest shred of honour?' His words were rough with desire, broken with fervour. 'I've hurt you so badly already, and you're sore and stiff and aching from your ordeal in the *maquis*.' He rocked her in his arms, unconsciously aping the comfort given to a child, but his vital male body was already responding to the warm, hardening curves that reached to him for solace, as Alex had prayed it would.

'Then make me better,' she whispered. 'Love me, Alain!'

'I can't!'

Giselle had said he never showed pain, but now his features were contorted by the strength of some inner agony. 'Not until you know the truth—and then you won't want me near you!'

CHAPTER ELEVEN

STOICALLY Alex absorbed the stab of pain which scythed through her, more hurtful than any of the punishing thorns which had ripped her tender skin.

'I know you still love Claudine, if that's what you mean,' she admitted wearily. Probably now he'd despise her for being willing to play the part of second best in his life, or consider her willingness to do so only increased her venality.

'Claudine?' He seemed genuinely taken aback, his eyes flexing in surprise. 'No, that's not true. I never loved Claudine any more than she did me. I may have hidden my true feelings from you, but I never lied about Claudine! Time and events threw us together; she appeared to like me and it wasn't long before our names were linked together. When Dubois called me to one side and suggested she and I announce our engagement on her twentieth birthday, she was willing, and it seemed a sensible thing to do at the time.'

'Sensible?' Alex felt as if she were dreaming, convinced by his whole attitude that he was indeed telling her the truth but amazed by it.

Alain shrugged his shoulders. 'I was in my thirties and beginning to think for the first time of domesticity—perhaps because of the ideal example Giselle was setting me. I argued that just because my father's marriage had been so traumatic it didn't mean I couldn't build a successful future for myself with a woman. Claudine seemed ideal—young, pretty and with all the right connections and background. I was fond of her, and presumably she found me just as eligible since she agreed to her father's suggestion.' He paused, then added thoughtfully, 'You see, I wanted a home and family of my own to return to after a day in the city. I wanted children and the chance to show them all the love and devotion I felt I'd been denied...'

'I understand,' she whispered, shocked and touched by his honesty, her hand reaching for his, offering her friendship because it was a driving compulsion, uncaring whether it was accepted or not.

'It was the perfect arranged marriage so beloved of moneyed classes the world over: suitable, apt and con-venient——' to her gratification he returned the pressure of her clasp '—but without that elusive ingredient I'd never really hoped to discover—love!'

'And then she ran off without a word—knowing you'd already bought a home for her——' Indignation had forced Alex's interjection.

'No.' He stopped her outburst, a flicker of amusement warming his eyes, whether at her own outrage or some inner memory of his own she couldn't be sure. 'No,' he repeated, his eyes darkening further with an unexpected warmth. 'You're taking events out of sequence. *Then* I met *you*—Alex Hammond, young, blonde, beautiful and totally unaware of who or what I was—and it was an encounter that turned my life upside-down. For the first time I was filled with terrible doubts. If I intended to settle down with Claudine surely I shouldn't be experi-encing the painful emotions which assaulted me as our work threw us more and more together? I knew so little about you—and had no right to find out more! All I knew was you were lovely to look at, always beautifully and expensively dressed, liked by all your colleagues... and my pulses beat like a teenager's every time you came near me!'

She was clearly delirious. Alex closed her eyes momentarily, easing her body against the comfort of the pillows, hearing Alain declare an irresistible attraction for her, and knowing it couldn't be real. The *maquis* could be poisonous, she knew that, but she wouldn't admit to her hallucinations in case he found some drug to alleviate them. She would enjoy the illusions while they lasted.

'By the time I had to go to Bradford I was quite hopelessly in love with you, but not prepared to admit it to myself because I was honour-bound to keep my promise to Claudine, and then, a few days later, Giselle phoned me with the news of her elopement. I should have been hurt and angry!' His voice deepened, took on an abrasive edge as he turned his own hand so that it rested palm to palm with her own. 'First my mother then Claudine throwing me over—what was wrong with me as a human being—a man?' Bitterness laced his words as he tore aside yet another of the veils which had shielded his vanity, exposing the core of his sensitivity to her. 'But it wasn't long before I realised that the very real pain I felt had nothing to do with Claudine—only to do with the breaking of an impossible dream, sharing my life with a loving, caring woman who would be the mother of my children, the keystone of my future.'

'Oh—Alain...' He wouldn't want pity and she was careful not to let him see how close she was to tears on his behalf. This was a dream she would preserve as long as possible...

'Then into the darkness of that moment came a vision—*you*, and I was caught up in a wild excitement. Released from any responsibility I'd felt for Claudine, I recognised the true power of what I felt for you. *Un coup de foudre!* Love at first sight! As a hard-headed banker, I should have mocked the idea. Incredibly I couldn't.'

Dry-mouthed, Alex forced herself to sit upright, keeping her mounting joy under control, reminding herself there was no happy ending to this story, somewhere along the way something had gone terribly wrong. But he had loved her once! She hadn't been mistaken!

'I phoned you as soon as I returned to London, suffering the agonies of the damned when there was no reply all night,' he went on speaking in a low, compulsive voice, his face shadowed with emotion. 'Were you with a lover? What kind of competition did I have? You weren't very forthcoming with information,' a wry grin transformed the angular lines of his face for a brief moment, 'but what I did find out didn't please me! It seemed you had a lover called Tony with whom you spent weekends and who had first call on your leisure time, and you clearly resented my interest in the matter—although you did tell me he couldn't give you what you wanted out of life, which gave me a chance, however slim!' He grimaced, pulling the corners of his attractive mouth downwards. 'Also on the credit side, there was this chemical buzz between us—I was sure that you felt it too.'

Dumbly Alex nodded. Yes, she had felt it but failed to recognise its deeper meaning—until later. But Alain had known *then*; fighting against time and unknown rivals, he had made a determined assault to achieve his aims.

'So you wooed me with a mixture of charm, high-handedness and shock tactics?' She returned his smile, remembering events.

'There was no time for subtlety,' he admitted shamelessly. 'Any day I would have to return to Paris and that would increase my task a thousandfold! So I used whatever tools I could lay hands on, including a certain amount of managerial blackmail. Oh, yes, you opposed me,' his eyes sparkled with the light of a battle enjoyed, 'but it was the opposition of magnets dragging against each other. I realised that you were reacting to me, that there was a powerful sexual attraction between us. More on my part—but I would settle for what I could get and work on the rest of it.

'Hell! I had a lot to offer a woman in status and material goods...' He stared at her, his gaze clear. 'It didn't matter to me what secrets your past held as long as I would be your future. I managed to persuade myself that once you were my wife I could make you love me...' He swallowed with difficulty. 'And then when I held you in my arms and felt your response I knew the time was right to ask you...'

'I did love you,' she told him sadly. So what had gone wrong? In retrospect she thought she knew. What he'd felt for her had never been love, just infatuation. If he hadn't had such a traumatised childhood, if only they'd had a longer time together, she could have discovered earlier that he had mistakenly cast her as his dream girl—a figment of his imagination. Her rival had been far more powerful than Claudine. She'd been an insubstantial vision no flesh and blood could ever hope to emulate!

Still determined to keep her sawing emotions under control so as not to add to his embarrassment, Alex swallowed hard on the rising lump in her throat, knowing as he rose to his feet and moved with an inherent masculine grace towards the unshuttered window, gazing out into the silent night, that this was the part which was going to hurt most of all. Automatically, her fists closed, her nails clamping hard against her tender palms, as he began to speak.

'Yes, I see now that you did—and I threw it all away because I allowed all my hopes and aspirations to be demolished in a few brief moments...' The silence stretched between them almost tangible in its oppressive power, and then he spoke again, the words exploding against her comprehension like bullets.

'You see, I believed you were pregnant with Tony Gibson's child. I was convinced, on our wedding-day, that you'd married me to escape the results of your indiscretions—no need to admit to your best friend that you'd made love with her husband, no need to consider an abortion, no need to kill the child of the man you loved... I would provide you with everything you wanted—a husband, a father for your child, a home and respectability!'

Shock paralysed Alex into immobility as the words seemed to echo round the room, bouncing back unintelligibly from the walls, as Alain remained where he was, back rigid, thighs taut, his face resolutely turned away from her.

Into the extended silence she laughed. A burst of sound half incredulous, half hysterical, an uncontrollable emission she couldn't control as her diaphragm heaved with effort.

'Stop it!' White-faced, Alain came to her, grabbing her by the arms. 'Don't laugh at me, Alex. I could cope with your having had a lover. I was so besotted with you I wouldn't even have condemned you out of hand for making love with your best friend's husband. I couldn't have condoned it either, but for the first time in my life I was beginning to understand how passions get out of control. I would have even admired you for not trying to break up their marriage... What I couldn't forgive was your agreeing to marry me without telling me about it. I thought you intended to pass the child off as mine, that you were using me as a convenient escape from a desperate situation—and I felt as if I were being crucified!'

Anguish tortured his face, pulling the muscles into spasm as the laughter died from Alex's throat. There were still questions to be asked, but so much was already becoming clear—the way he'd deferred consummating their union, attempting no doubt to coerce her into admitting what she'd done. How long had he intended to ignore her? A month or two perhaps, until her supposed condition became clear and she was forced to

break her silence? But it hadn't worked out like that...he
had wanted her too much...

An appalling thought struck her. 'You don't still believe it, do you?'

'You were a virgin.' He choked the words out, and
she could feel the tension in his body, the force of
adrenalin quickening his heartbeat and causing his
muscles to tremble with suppressed strength. 'And that's
just one more debit in the ledger! Heaven knows what
I put you through this morning. By the time I'd realised
the extent of my sins and recovered any signs of lucidity
you'd fallen asleep beside me—my warm, beautiful, innocent Alex—your body hot and flushed offered without
conditions to the monster you'd taken as a husband!

'I showered and dressed and went downstairs to try
and create some kind of order out of the chaos of my
thoughts, to make plans as how best to make reparation
to you. Then when I went to look for you, you'd
disappeared.' His voice thickened. 'I'd expected to lose
you—it was no more than I deserved—but not like
that...not driven out into the *maquis* like a criminal
when I was the only one to have committed a crime.'
He lowered his head in the soft curve of her neck and
shoulder, as she nestled her cheek against his crisp hair,
her arms encompassing him, hands stroking his back in
long, soothing strokes, maternal rather than loverlike.

'But I still don't really understand; there must have
been some reason why you thought what you did,' she
said softly, puzzled. 'Tony and I were never anything
but friends. We'd known each other since we were
children. He's like a brother to me. It never occurred to
me that you would suspect us of being anything else,
especially as I introduced you to him and Martine at the
wedding as a happily married couple.' Her blue eyes
widened with distress. 'You greeted them both with every
sign of friendship...'

He stirred in her arms. 'Because I never suspected then that it was the same man. After all, it's not an uncommon name and I'd never dreamed you would invite an ex-lover to your wedding. Besides, he and Martine seemed so ideally happy...' He sighed heavily. 'I'd like to say I wasn't jealous of your former liaisons but it wouldn't be true. I couldn't claim total chastity for myself—like most young men, I'd had relationships in the past, but their very emptiness had made them pall. Recently there'd been no one, certainly not Claudine. But, even against my instincts, I had to accord you the same rights. I didn't want to put a face or name to my rival, then or ever. I'd made up my mind that I'd never question you about him again.'

Still puzzled, Alex tightened her hold round Alain's firm body, encouraging his confidences. 'So what changed your mind?'

She felt rather than heard the deep breath he drew. 'Something upset you at the reception. I looked across the room and you were crying. I saw Tony Gibson put his arm around you and lead you away. Naturally I followed; I was afraid you were ill...'

'Just missing my parents on my wedding-day,' she admitted as he paused, frowning as she tried to recall what had happened next. She and Tony had gone into the small bar behind the main reception-room and sat talking, touching on their friendship... Then they'd gone on to discuss Martine's forthcoming operation and the possibility of having a baby. They'd mentioned making the right decision, giving the child a good home... She'd even said something about being with Tony at the christening... The exact words eluded her, but the nucleus of their meaning was crystal-clear.

'I overheard your conversation,' Alain admitted painfully. 'Or at least part of it. It seemed to me that there was only one possible conclusion to draw from it.' He swallowed deeply. 'I felt—devastated. The revelation that he had been the man in your life and that you still cared deeply for him was bad enough—but when he mentioned a baby——' His voice broke on the last word.

'I remember.' Alex's tender fingers continued with their soothing journey across the tense muscles of his back, as she fought back the horror that threatened to overwhelm her. 'Oh, not every word, but the gist of it.'

Gently she told him the dilemma facing her friends, the tragedies Martine had already suffered, and her own part in their story. She shivered as her voice faded away to a whisper on the final words.

The past days had been dreadful, but if it had been any other man but Alain they could have been a great deal worse! Another man labouring under the same bizarre misapprehension might have thrashed her or even murdered her! If she'd ever had doubts about the extent of his love for her, the restraint he'd shown was a powerful advocate on his behalf, and with that knowledge a powerful joy was stirring deep within her. Alain had always cared for her...

He stirred in her hold and she let him go. 'I love you, Alex; I always did. It was an instinct which laughed at logic. If you only knew how often I've stared at that portrait you had done in Montmartre, torn by terrible doubts, because what I believed was so totally opposed to the qualities the artist had seen in your face. The qualities that condemned me as a victim of some incomprehensible misunderstanding—or mad! I should have trusted you. Now I don't even have the arrogance to beg your forgiveness.'

'But apart from anything else you believed I'd only married you for what you could give me.' She forced the words out between stiff lips, as the memory of his accusation returned to haunt her.

'No, regardless of what I said, I never believed that,' he denied it sadly. 'But when I discovered, or thought I had, that you were expecting another man's child I had to protect myself. I daren't let you see how completely I'd become enmeshed in your spell, what a fool you'd made of me, so I pretended that from the start I'd seen our marriage as a business arrangement on both sides.' He expelled his breath in a harsh sigh. 'I used whatever ammunition I could dredge up from the past, insubstantial though it was, to make a case against you in order to salve my own pride. It was the only way I could see at the time to strike back at you when my whole world was dissolving around me.'

'But you weren't prepared to accuse me directly about what you believed?' she asked wonderingly. 'Oh, Alain— it could have been cleared up so easily!'

But even as she asked the question and saw the shake of his head she knew how impossibly painful such a direct confrontation would have been for him.

'I would never have let you go, you know,' he told her quietly. 'I would have looked after you and the baby, but not in apparent ignorance. I needed you to confide in me, respect me enough to tell me what I believed to be the truth.' He shuddered. 'Then in the end my love for you was too great. I had to possess you whatever the price to my self-esteem. *Dieu!* When I think what a fool I was. Suppose you hadn't been a virgin, or I'd been too insensitive to realise how innocent you were—my paranoia could have destroyed us both!'

'No.' Alex spoke swiftly to reassure him, to prevent his self-anger from intensifying. 'No, that would never have happened, because in time everything would have become clear. Tony and Martine are my friends. I would have talked about them, you would have learned of their problems, you couldn't have helped but realise there'd been a terrible misunderstanding—but this was the best way, my love, because it was the quickest, and now everything's cleared up between us we can go ahead and enjoy the rest of our honeymoon, can't we?' She invited his collusion with a tender smile of invitation.

'You're saying you can forgive me for everything I've said and done since we became man and wife?' He stared at her in disbelief. 'That you could still find it in your heart to love me after everything that's happened?'

'I'm saying I never stopped loving you,' she told him honestly. 'Even when I thought I was a poor substitute for Claudine.'

'I don't know what to say...' The words choked in his throat and she saw the knuckles of his clenched fists whiten, the enormity of his distress a barrier between them.

'But you know what to do,' she suggested gently.

'Are you sure?'

Entranced, she read desire maturing in the depth of his amber eyes, and responded to it with a tender smile. 'Of course.' The sting of her wounds was long forgotten in the euphoria that possessed her. 'I want to become as experienced as you thought I was!'

For a moment she wondered if she'd been wrong to tease him, if apparently ignoring his anguish would insult him, then she saw his beautiful mouth curve into a smile of pure happiness and relief.

'That's fine by me, *ma chère* Alex, provided I'm your only tutor.'

'Now and forever,' she agreed joyously, opening her arms to receive him, hugging him to her, glorying in the feel of his physical arousal and the deep knowledge that she was going to fill the gap in his life with all the love and stability he could possibly crave from her.

'Alex, *je t'adore*...' They were the last words spoken for a very long time.

Fourteen days later she walked steadily along the narrow cliff track, avoiding the occasional file of large dark ants which scurried across the path. Beneath her feet the perfume of crushed leaves rose to greet her; above her the sun pulsated in an azure sky, licking at her skin with a ferocious tongue. Ahead of her Alain moved with an easy, controlled stride adapted to her own slower pace.

Tomorrow the honeymoon would be over and they would return to Paris. These incredible hours of hot days and warm, loving nights in an idyllic setting would be ended.

The prospect of living in Paris and being Alain's wife with all it entailed was a heady one, sure as she was that the closeness which had grown between them would continue to flourish when they left the lush and beautiful setting of Corsica.

Without warning her foot caught on a stone and she stumbled, sending a shower of stones rattling down the sheer cliff. Alain spun around, concern on his face.

'What happened? Did you hurt yourself?'

'No, I'm fine.' She smiled at his worried face. 'I'll be glad when we find some shade and I can get in the water though! I feel dreadfully overdressed!'

A reluctant grin turned the corners of his mouth. 'It's for your own sake, my love.' He touched the long-sleeved light cotton blouse he'd insisted on her wearing over a full cotton skirt. 'However tanned you are, your skin is too fair to take this kind of hammering from the sun.'

'Yes, I know.' Alex grinned ruefully, taking off her sun-hat and waving it in front of her face, trying to stir the still air. 'Is it much further?'

How she envied Alain his Latin skin, the long, beautifully tanned legs which he could expose to the sun beneath cut-off denim shorts with only a glistening coat of sun oil to baffle the ultra-violet-ray bombardment. Yet he too had shown wisdom in covering his back and shoulders with a light cotton shirt.

It had been her idea to do something different on their last day, so, when Alain had diffidently suggested walking to the a deserted beach along the coast, she'd readily agreed.

'Five minutes.' He pointed ahead to where the cliff path turned and dropped. 'Do you want a drink now?' He hoisted the large plastic container he was carrying away from his shoulder.

Alex shook her head. 'No, I'll wait. It'll taste all the sweeter for the waiting.'

They exchanged knowing, intimate smiles, and Alex was glad her eyes were shielded by dark glasses because the declaration of her love would have been so blatant it would have blinded him!

They found shade at last, sinking down beneath giant rocks, drinking their water, stripping off their outer clothes to plunge and frolic in a sea as quiet and still as a pool of mercury.

Sitting beside Alain afterwards, Alex stole a look at her husband, long arms encircling bent knees, his darkly handsome profile turned slightly away, his sombre eyes narrowed and brooding, and felt her skin prickle as she sensed a deep unhappiness.

Tentatively she touched his bronzed forearm and felt him start.

'Sorry, Alex. I was years away.'

'Don't you mean miles?' she queried with amusement.

He shook his head. 'No. I was thinking of this place twenty-five years ago.'

'When you were nine?' Her eyebrows rose in surprise.

He nodded. 'We used to come here for holidays. Papa, Giselle and the woman who used to care for us. We stayed in a small hotel about four miles down the coast.' He pointed away from the direction of the villa. 'Usually it was for about four weeks every year, but on this particular occasion my school reports had been pretty horrific, and Papa had arranged for me to have private tuition. It meant I could only stay for one week; after that Giselle and the nanny would stay on, but my father and I would return to Avignon.' He laughed without humour. 'Can you imagine the misery of a nine-year-old boy having to leave this place after only a week?'

She nodded in silent sympathy. Probably his father had thought he was acting for the best—but for the young boy...

'Anyway, I had this plan,' he continued evenly. 'I waited until the evening we were due to leave and I ran away. I came to this beach. In those days an old peasant lived in that tumbled-down house we passed on our way here. He kept chickens and grew vegetables and I fancied I could get something to eat until Papa gave up looking for me and went back to Avignon by himself.'

'What happened?' she asked quietly, sensing the onset of catastrophe.

Naked shoulders rose in resignation. 'He found me, of course. Giselle knew where I was and they got it out of her.' He smiled a slow, reminiscent smile that turned her heart. 'He came for me by himself. It was the early hours of the following day and I was barely awake when he rolled me off the mattress I'd made of seaweed, took off his belt and thrashed me till I could hardly stand.'

He spoke quietly, but after a quarter of a century the desolation was a living presence in his voice. Unable to speak, Alex dropped her head on to the sweet brown silk of his shoulder, totally unable to control her tears.

'Alex?' She was conscious of his surprise. 'Alex, don't cry! I deserved everything I got—just think of the fuss, the panic, missed planes, cancelled appointments my actions caused. Alex...?' His arm tightened convulsively round her shoulders.

'I'm sorry.' She brushed away the tears, subduing the scalding grief she felt for the child torn from his sister and the place he loved, beaten for his sins and facing the long walk over the cliffs with his stern and silent parent. 'Alain, did it ever occur to you your father might have been so harsh with you, not because of all the trouble you caused, but because he thought he'd lost you forever—because he loved you?'

He was silent for so long she thought her words had fallen on deaf ears, then he said softly, 'Not till a long time later. Not, in fact, until I thought you'd run away from me and I'd lost the most precious thing in my life. When I heard your voice calling for help and I knew you were safe my first instinct was to beat you black and blue until you cried for mercy!'

'Oh!' It wasn't quite the response she'd expected, but it served her purpose.

'Don't worry.' He cast her a sidelong glance. 'I could never hurt you, *ma chérie;* besides, nature had already made you pay for your escapade.' He touched one of the remaining scars on her leg with a gentle finger, his lips twisting in wry sympathy. 'But, yes, for the first time in my life I could see the connection between love and violence, abhorrent though I still find the practice.'

'So,' she persevered, 'if your father wanted to see you, if he was prepared to come to Paris and meet you, you'd play your part in trying to heal the breach between you?'

'You think there's a possibility that might happen?' She'd expected a downright refusal, but there was plenty in his manner that gave her hope, a gleam of expectation in the clear oloroso eyes that thrilled her.

'A very definite possibility, my love,' she assured him. 'After all, you've got a wife now and the possibility—probability—of continuing the du Gard dynasty. Giselle tells me that your father has mellowed over the years—and that he's always cared deeply for you despite his inability to make that obvious to you. As for me, I think the time has come to forget old wrongs—all of them.'

'I agree.' He reached for her, leaning across her body, caressing her mouth with warm, searching kisses. 'Forgive us our trespasses, hmm? I would be very proud indeed to introduce him to his new daughter-in-law.'

The beach was deserted, the ancient house on its outskirts empty and crumbling, the nearest human being five miles away in a vertical direction, coasting the heavens in a Boeing 747. In a setting made for romance the brilliant Gallic financier took his wife in his arms, and loved her with a grace and power and tenderness and total disregard for propriety she would remember all her life.

Towards the end of the afternoon they started on the long walk back to the villa so tightly embraced they walked as one. At the top of the cliff Alain turned to look down at the solitary beach.

'So much pain,' he said slowly. 'And now so much pleasure. It feels as if I've exorcised a ghost here today.'

Alex's arm tightened round him in quick understanding. 'My feelings are so mixed too, Alain. I feel so happy and yet so sad as well because we're going to leave the summer and all its magic behind us when we leave tomorrow.'

'But we're not!' Quickly he contradicted her. 'We're taking the summer and everything it's given us back to Paris with us. We're never going to let it end now we've discovered it together, Alex—never!'

A life of endless summer. He was right. It sounded good. Happily Alex tucked her arm inside her husband's and matched his stride as they set off together on the homeward path.

HARLEQUIN
Romance

A Christmas tradition...

Imagine spending Christmas in New Orleans with a blind stranger and his aged guide dog—when you're supposed to be there on your honeymoon!
#3163 Every Kind of Heaven
by Bethany Campbell

Imagine spending Christmas with a man you once "married"—in a mock ceremony at the age of eight!
#3166 The Forgetful Bride
by Debbie Macomber

Available in December 1991, wherever Harlequin books are sold.

RXM

"INDULGE A LITTLE" SWEEPSTAKES

HERE'S HOW THE SWEEPSTAKES WORKS

NO PURCHASE NECESSARY

To enter each drawing, complete the appropriate Official Entry Form or a 3" by 5" index card by hand-printing your name, address and phone number and the trip destination that the entry is being submitted for (i.e., Walt Disney World Vacation Drawing, etc.) and mailing it to: Indulge '91 Subscribers-Only Sweepstakes, P.O. Box 1397, Buffalo, New York 14269-1397.

No responsibility is assumed for lost, late or misdirected mail. Entries must be sent separately with first class postage affixed, and be received by: 9/30/91 for the Walt Disney World Vacation Drawing, 10/31/91 for the Alaskan Cruise Drawing and 11/30/91 for the Hawaiian Vacation Drawing. Sweepstakes is open to residents of the U.S. and Canada, 21 years of age or older as of 11/7/91.

For complete rules, send a self-addressed, stamped (WA residents need not affix return postage) envelope to: Indulge '91 Subscribers-Only Sweepstakes Rules, P.O. Box 4005, Blair, NE 68009.

© 1991 HARLEQUIN ENTERPRISES LTD.

DIR-RL

"INDULGE A LITTLE" SWEEPSTAKES

HERE'S HOW THE SWEEPSTAKES WORKS

NO PURCHASE NECESSARY

To enter each drawing, complete the appropriate Official Entry Form or a 3" by 5" index card by hand-printing your name, address and phone number and the trip destination that the entry is being submitted for (i.e., Walt Disney World Vacation Drawing, etc.) and mailing it to: Indulge '91 Subscribers-Only Sweepstakes, P.O. Box 1397, Buffalo, New York 14269-1397.

No responsibility is assumed for lost, late or misdirected mail. Entries must be sent separately with first class postage affixed, and be received by: 9/30/91 for the Walt Disney World Vacation Drawing, 10/31/91 for the Alaskan Cruise Drawing and 11/30/91 for the Hawaiian Vacation Drawing. Sweepstakes is open to residents of the U.S. and Canada, 21 years of age or older as of 11/7/91.

For complete rules, send a self-addressed, stamped (WA residents need not affix return postage) envelope to: Indulge '91 Subscribers-Only Sweepstakes Rules, P.O. Box 4005, Blair, NE 68009.

© 1991 HARLEQUIN ENTERPRISES LTD.

DIR-RL

INDULGE A LITTLE—WIN A LOT!

Summer of '91 Subscribers-Only Sweepstakes

OFFICIAL ENTRY FORM

This entry must be received by: Nov. 30, 1991
This month's winner will be notified by: Dec. 7, 1991
Trip must be taken between: Jan. 7, 1992—Jan. 7, 1993

YES, I want to win the 3-Island Hawaiian vacation for two. I understand the prize includes round-trip airfare, first-class hotels and pocket money as revealed on the "wallet" scratch-off card.

Name _____

Address_____ Apt. _____

City _____

State/Prov. _____ Zip/Postal Code _____

Daytime phone number _____
(Area Code)

Return entries with invoice in envelope provided. Each book in this shipment has two entry coupons—and the more coupons you enter, the better your chances of winning!

© 1991 HARLEQUIN ENTERPRISES LTD.   3R-CPS

INDULGE A LITTLE—WIN A LOT!

Summer of '91 Subscribers-Only Sweepstakes

OFFICIAL ENTRY FORM

This entry must be received by: Nov. 30, 1991
This month's winner will be notified by: Dec. 7, 1991
Trip must be taken between: Jan. 7, 1992—Jan. 7, 1993

YES, I want to win the 3-Island Hawaiian vacation for two. I understand the prize includes round-trip airfare, first-class hotels and pocket money as revealed on the "wallet" scratch-off card.

Name _____

Address_____ Apt. _____

City _____

State/Prov. _____ Zip/Postal Code _____

Daytime phone number _____
(Area Code)

Return entries with invoice in envelope provided. Each book in this shipment has two entry coupons—and the more coupons you enter, the better your chances of winning!

© 1991 HARLEQUIN ENTERPRISES LTD.   3R-CPS